# DARK
# REIGN

# DARK REIGN

DARKHAVEN SAGA: BOOK NINE

## DANIELLE ROSE

WATERHOUSE PRESS

*For June*

# ONE

Distorted pictures, jumbled and messy, flash before my eyes. With each blink, I see something new, something raw and real.

I see my friends in pools of blood—some are awake, others unmoving.

I see Holland. With ancient texts surrounding him, the witch cradles his lover in his arms, clutching Jeremiah's head to his chest. Holland sways from side to side, cooing softly.

Sound is still muffled, like those who speak do so with hands around their throats. Voices are hoarse and scratchy—their tone utterly unfamiliar. Color is blinding and bright. Our blood, a stagnant stench of rusted metal, is all-consuming. Everything about this place reeks of death.

I am lying on the floor, staring at the wood grain. My head is pounding, and each pulsating beat feels like a hundred tiny knives carving into my skull, but I am no jack-o'-lantern, and this is not a joyous occasion. Still, the ache is rooted so deeply, the sensation so pure and true, I feel it in my brain.

I hack each time I breathe, like even my lungs are protesting my survival. I tell myself I need to get up, to fight, to protect my friends, but my limbs object. My body convulses with each muscle spasm. Everything feels tight and overworked from constant strain. My muscles twinge when I attempt to move, and I feel the groan from deep within, as though even my bones are brittle.

Still, I manage to push myself off the floor, using all my strength to sit upright. My arms feel heavy, and my legs tingle, like the blood hasn't yet reached my extremities. The sensation is overpowering, and it is all I can think about for several long moments.

Only when the tiny prickling ceases do I realize I am dizzy, and it takes several seconds to regain my composure. My skin is clammy, my chest tight. I focus on inhaling slowly, on holding each breath, on exhaling long and deep. I never stop shaking.

I think I almost died.

When I finally see clearly, I am greeted by the destruction Sofía caused. It is everything I feared, everything I warned the others about—yet it is so much worse than I could have ever imagined.

The hunters are wounded, with crimson streaks cascading from their eyes and ears.

I scratch at my own skin, and blood cakes my fingernails. I wipe away the evidence on my face, only to have hands stained in red. I should be used to such a sight, but it is no less startling.

Jeremiah still hasn't woken, but the others begin to shift.

Hikari crawls closer, her fingers scraping against the floorboards. The sound radiates through the wood and vibrates against my legs. Her usually spiky hair is smooth against one side of her head, where she must have slept on it. The other side stands on end, much like the hackles down my spine.

Only now do I realize how uneasy I feel in this weakened state. Anything can happen, and I wouldn't be able to protect myself—or the others. I need to feed, to rest, but I fear I haven't the time.

Malik is still lying on his back, but he angles his head

toward me. Our gazes meet, and I hold my breath, taking in the sight of my leader. His eyes are pooled with tears. They free-fall, and the longer they water, the clearer the liquid becomes. What was once a deep, bright red is now a pale, light pink. He wipes his eyes with the back of his hand and turns over, clawing to sit upright.

"Please wake up," Holland whispers, catching the attention of everyone in the room.

Cradling Jeremiah in his arms, the witch repeats his plea over and over again. Jeremiah doesn't stir, but I know he is not dead, for if he were dead, he would be ash. But like the rest of us, he is simply broken and bruised.

As my body begins to slowly heal from the assault, I assess each hunter, gaze settling on my friends for only seconds at a time.

This is it. This is everyone. The fate of Darkhaven rests in our hands, and I hate to admit it, but we have seen better days.

Against a rogue militia, we are outnumbered and outmatched. We face a superior threat armed with my amulet. I try to remain strong, but like spilled blood on fresh soil, doubt seeps in, spreading until what was once lush and fertile is now drenched in gore. I fear I will forever be haunted by my past mistakes.

Jeremiah groans loudly, his wail echoing around the otherwise silent room. It bounces off the walls and pierces my heart—yet another dagger to flesh I am forced to bear. I release the breath I was holding only to suck in another lungful of air. It is loud and sharp, and it forces the others to look at me.

Jeremiah mumbles something inaudible, and Holland pulls him closer. The wounded vampire moans in protest, likely feeling the intense weakness I experienced when I first woke. My body is healing now, and as each second passes, I grow stronger—and hungrier.

"What happened?" Jeremiah asks, voice groggy, tone low and slow.

He raises his hand to his head, resting his fingers against his temple to ease what is undoubtedly one heck of a tension headache. Without realizing, he smears the blood that cascades down his sharp angles, from cheekbone to jawline, giving it the eerie illusion of war paint. He has yet to open his eyes, to witness the devastation firsthand. He has no idea that we were imprisoned in our own bloodbath.

"Sofía," I hiss.

"What did she do?" Hikari asks, still dazed. She sits on her knees, bottom resting firmly against the heels of her feet. Still, she wobbles, failing to steady herself.

I experienced that same dizziness when I pushed myself up from the floor. The wave of nausea that followed only solidifies our predicament, our frailty.

Hikari squeezes her eyes shut and murmurs under her breath, but when she scratches at her scalp, hands brushing over the untextured hair on just one side of her head, she frowns.

"How long were we out?" she adds.

"I'm not sure," I admit. "But it feels like my brain exploded."

Using the pads of my fingers, I rub circles across my forehead with both hands, hoping to find that perfect spot that eases the ensuing migraine. Unfortunately, I am offered no such reprieve, but I don't stop. The awareness of skin-on-skin contact is a decent distraction. It makes me feel like a hunter again—like I wasn't recently demoted from predator to prey.

"I imagine that is exactly what she tried to do," Malik says.

"She used her magic to...what? Blow us up from the inside?" Hikari asks. "How is that even possible?"

"After everything we have experienced, I am beginning to realize there is very little we can deem truly impossible."

"We're lucky," I say. "Our vampire abilities saved our lives."

"Are we?" Hikari asks. Malik shoots her a glare, but she ignores him. "Sofía is a powerful witch. I can't imagine she'd mess up a spell as important as this."

"You're right," I say. "If she wanted to eliminate us, she would have. She just needed us out of the way."

"So she'll be back?" Hikari asks.

"She'll be back," I agree.

Malik sniffles and wipes away a drop of blood from his nostril. Normally buzzed close to his scalp, his hair has grown out a little bit longer. Since I have known him, he has favored the military style—in both appearance and warcraft—so he now appears disheveled.

All the little things I failed to notice before—from Malik's overgrown hair to Hikari's tired eyes... They mock me now. I was too busy worrying about myself—about how I alone would save the world—to notice my friends' distress.

I need to be better. I need to grow up.

Holland helps Jeremiah sit upright, but even after he does, he never loosens his grasp on the vampire. Instead, he stares into his lover's eyes and begs for forgiveness. He repeats his apology over and over again, drawing frowns from everyone in the room.

"You have nothing to be sorry about," Jeremiah whispers.

His voice cracks, but already, he sounds stronger. He is

healing, and with newfound health, he will require sustenance. We all will, but our supply is dangerously low.

"I didn't even try to stop her," Holland admits.

I don't miss his shame; it coats his words, somehow thickening the sound, like a strong accent or a heavy drawl. I feel the weight of his confession like iron compressed to my chest.

I know his agony. I too have felt regret for missed opportunities, and it is as painful as death by stoning. My mishaps resulted in the annihilation of an entire coven, of the theft of an amulet that should not exist. I am desperate to ease his pain.

"You couldn't have stopped her," I say, speaking only the truth. "She is more powerful than even you, Holland."

I am blunt, but I need to be. I can only hope my words cut through his remorse.

"But I didn't even try!" Holland says, his voice a shriek. "I saw what she did, what she was doing to you all, and instead of saving my friends, I focused all my energy on protecting those stupid books and that damn orb."

"You did the right thing," Malik says.

Our leader is cool and calm. He is collected even though I am certain he too wants to break.

"If she left with the amulet and the books, we would never complete the sun spell," he adds. "We wouldn't be able to stop them."

"I know, but..."

"The choices we make are rarely easy," Malik says. "But do not allow your emotions to overtake your mind. You know you made the right decision. Those relics cannot protect themselves. We can."

I am seated on my bottom, my knees pulled to my chest, watching the water swirl down the drain, and the longer I stare at it, the easier it is to pretend it is something else entirely. I imagine it is crimson and thick. It is easy to see a river of blood everywhere I look because carnage is all I know. I was born into this war, and I made it my life.

I can think about nothing else except for the loss of my sire. Malik says I should know if he is okay. I should feel the exact moment he is taken from this world. So I try to connect to him. My soul reaches out, searching for that mystical tether we have always seemed to have, but I find nothing. The astral plane where our connection was formed is expansive and barren, and he is not there.

I bury my face between my knees and close my eyes, no longer wanting to see red. Tears burn behind my lids. I allow them to fall freely, because as they mix with the waterfall above that cascades over my body, it is easy to pretend I am not losing control.

It is easier to break down when someone is here to catch me, but the hand that has always been here when I am led astray is gone. And his absence, his silence in these dire times, is deafening.

I say his name, and it sounds foreign on my tongue. I whisper it again, and a shudder worms its way through my torso. I feel like I am forgetting the way he looked, the way he sounded, the way his skin felt against mine.

I know that cannot be true.

He hasn't been gone long, but I struggle to remember the way my name graced his lips. Every second of the unknown feels like an eternity, a cruel fate for a creature granted just that. I refuse to spend the next several hundred years wishing I had done something differently.

I want him to be alive. I need him to be alive, but I try not to think about what that means, about the torment he is facing at the hands of our enemy. I remind myself that I know my father, and if he plans to use Jasik to sway me to the other side, he would not kill him. Papá is no fool. A dead vampire will only bring an angry hybrid.

The water has long since run cold, so I stand and dry off. My reflection in the mirror mocks me. The vampire who stares back appears healthy and youthful, but I know the pain that resides just beneath her perfect exterior. Inside, she is dead.

I use my fingers to brush my hair, gaze never averting from her crimson irises. A deep sense of misery washes over me as I mourn the mortal I used to be. So much has changed since I transitioned. I have lost everything, everyone—and now I might lose *him*.

I dress, taking my time choosing each garment even though I know exactly what to wear. I put on my signature black attire—the ensemble that transitions easily between hunting rogues or loitering the manor.

Preparing for the inevitable fight, I sheath the dagger Jasik gave me, listening as the blade slides against the worn leather. Beneath my jacket, it is invisible to onlookers, but my T-shirt is thin, so I feel the cool metal against my breast.

The weapon was a family heirloom, passed down through generations, and it gives me comfort, like I can turn to it for strength as my world steadily crumbles.

Downstairs, I hand Holland the other text I purchased from Lunar Magic. The one that better educated me on the uses of the black onyx stone. His gaze drops to the worn, leather-bound cover, and he frowns, likely wondering why I have waited until now to turn it over.

"I bought this from the same occult shop in Darkhaven," I explain. "I doubt it'll have more information than the others we've been using, but it might help."

I leave the text with him, walking to the kitchen without waiting for a response. Inside that tome, they will discover the truth—that the crystal we nearly died to protect has the capabilities of curing vampirism.

I wonder if someone will take the cure. Maybe Jeremiah, because Holland is mortal. Maybe Hikari, who seems to have grown tired of the endless war-torn days. Maybe Malik, so he can finally lay down his weapon and rest. Or maybe Jasik and I will take it together, spending our final days aged and happy— if such a thing were possible.

My leader is standing in the kitchen, his towering frame illuminated by the moonlight streaming through the stained-glass windows. In the darkness, it is easy to convince myself that he is Jasik.

Even as he turns to me, steaming mug of blood in hand, I see my sire.

Malik smiles, soft but sincere, and strides toward me. But as he moves, weakened body teetering with each step, he morphs into the vampire who trained me for this life.

He is not my lover.

Malik is not Jasik.

"Are you okay?" he asks, voice soft, intent honest.

Poised and seemingly emotionless, Malik has always been difficult to read, but lately, I seem to understand the words he can't say. The silence between us is littered with letters, each forming sentences that knot in our throats, never escaping. The string of words is full of accusation and fear and bitterness. I know Malik loves me the way he loves all his nestmates, but he is also fully aware that none of this would have happened had Jasik not turned me into a vampire. Still, he doesn't blame me for the dissolution of Amicia's nest or for her death, even if he sometimes wants to.

"I've been better," I admit.

He hands me the mug of blood he has been holding, and I greedily gulp it down, slurping every last drop. I feel it spreading through my chest, warm and thick, rejuvenating what has been broken and bruised.

"Do you think he's okay?" I whisper.

Malik exhales sharply, breath long and slow. He doesn't want to lie to me, but he doesn't opt for honesty either. He simply says nothing. When I look at him, meeting his gaze, his jaw clenches shut, the tiny muscles in his cheeks bulging from the strain, as if he fears he might actually blurt the truth.

"I think he's okay," I say softly.

This time, when Malik smiles, it does not reach his eyes.

# TWO

Hours have passed, and we are no closer to having answers or rescuing Jasik.

I pace the parlor, the creaking floor beneath my feet a constant reminder that this house is empty, that we have lost nearly everyone we promised to protect.

Those who stayed behind after Amicia's demise have long since lost faith in our ability to continue her legacy, and I don't blame them. Only the other hunters and I remain, and I am starting to lose them too.

I watch Holland as I walk back and forth. I know he is aware that all eyes are on him, but I don't want him to catch my stare. I fear what my lack of confidence will do in such a dire situation. So I keep my gaze down, and the moment it lingers on his seated silhouette for even a second, I avert my eyes.

Instead, I glance at the book stacks.

I sniff the musty air.

I pump my clenched fists.

I listen to my overworked heart.

I do anything I can to distract my racing thoughts.

Holland is mumbling to himself as he scratches words onto a notepad. His pencil is chewed and short, the eraser nearly gone. The tiny pink bud at the end of his writing utensil is as flat as the hours are long. Time ticks by slowly—a cruel

11

punishment saved only for those granted an eternity—each stroke of the pendulum within the upstairs grandfather clock like the sharp bite of leather whipped against bare skin.

This is my cross to bear.

The witch straddles the slender wood between his index and middle finger and taps it mindlessly against the paper. Each strike radiates through my spine, jolting me upright, as if he is about to shout that he has figured it out, that everything will be okay.

But he hasn't.

And it won't be.

I am well aware that I am fighting a losing battle, and even if I were to win this war, I would do so with a river of blood in my wake. So much has been lost since I transitioned. How can I be deemed victorious if the cost was losing our nest, my coven, my friends? If the price I must pay to save my sire is to slay my father, I am no hero. I am merely a conqueror.

The conservatory connects to this room through a single open door. I stare into the solarium now, watching as the rays of moonlight that illuminate the darkened space flutter as the clouds shift as the wind blows. The sun-room is long and angular, with pathways that also connect to the sitting room and dining room. Beyond that, at the solarium's abrupt end, there is another doorway—one that leads to the garden out back.

I see them even from where I stand in the parlor. The headstones in the small plot are solid, erect, a crude reminder. They are cast alight in a dim glow, with a soft dew making the dark stone glisten like magic.

But there is no magic there. No life. There is only death and decay and the representation of something that no longer exists in the physical world. I like to believe that Amicia is watching over us now, but I fail to convince myself that she would be proud.

"How's it going?" Hikari asks.

She folds her arms over her chest as she stares down at Holland, who remains seated on the floor. Though she is only a few inches taller than five feet in height, she towers over him now. Her black pixie locks are shiny and spiky, catching the light every time her head dips lower to meet Holland's gaze. Her eyes narrow, brow furrows, and even though I am certain she doesn't mean to, she radiates disdain. I can't blame her. She is a vampire scorned—and I know a little something about that.

Holland closes his eyes and exhales slowly, loudly. When he opens them again, I see his resolve.

"As you can imagine, it isn't going well," he says pointedly.

"Maybe I can help," Hikari offers.

Her voice is high-pitched and overly cheerful. The unnatural squeak coats each word, betraying her feigned confidence.

"It would be spectacularly helpful if you just left me alone," Holland says. "The pacing, the nervous energy, the hovering... None of you are making this easier."

Jeremiah strides to his lover, and just before he sinks to his bottom, he glares at Hikari. His death-dagger vision is a clear warning. *Back off.* Hikari must understand his rather obvious hint, because she storms out of the room in a huff.

I see her plop on a chair in the nearby sitting room. I understand her frustration. I feel it too. But pressuring Holland will only hinder his ability to help us. And right now, he's all we have.

Jeremiah clasps his hand over Holland's, and only then do I notice how much the witch is shaking. I assumed tapping his pencil against his notepad was a quirk, a habitual tic, but now I am wondering if it was the result of his anxiousness. Perhaps even he believes we are doomed.

"What's wrong?" Jeremiah asks, voice soft and smooth.

In just two words, Holland's demeanor changes from defensive to lax. Jasik holds the same power over me, nearly controlling my mood with the simple croon of his velvet voice. I worry I may never hear it again.

"I'm scared," Holland says, voice breaking. "What if I can't do this?"

"Holland . . ." Jeremiah says, voice soft, tone in disbelief.

He pulls the witch into his embrace and kisses his temple, long and slow. When Jeremiah speaks again, he does so against his skin, never backing away as he cradles Holland in his arms.

"You're asking me to do something never done before," Holland says. "Something that very well might be impossible."

"I know you can do this. You can do anything you put your mind to."

"Why are you so sure?" Holland asks, pulling away from the vampire in order to look him in the eyes. "Why are you so confident I won't mess this up?"

"Because you are the strongest witch I know. If anyone can do this, if anyone can create magic where none exists, it's you. It doesn't matter if this has never been done before. You are strong and smart, and we would not ask this of someone incapable of summoning the magic needed to complete this spell. We believe in you. You just have to believe in yourself."

"You make it sound so simple," Holland says, smiling softly.

They kiss, brief but sincere, and as I watch their love unfold before me, I feel my own heart break. I ache for Jasik—physically and mentally and emotionally. I yearn for him, needing him in every way, and I am denied my reprieve again and again.

Unable to bear witness to what I so desperately want but cannot have, I turn away. As though my limb has a mind of its own, my hand moves to the empty space between my clavicle bones. My fingertips touch skin, the soft caress sending a shiver through my body. There is nothing there but exposed skin, bare and unprotected.

Secured in the hands of our enemy, the amulet is gone, but what leaves me on edge, what makes my skin prickle, is not what is missing. There is a tightness in my chest, an ache rooted so deeply in my gut, I feel it in my bones. A frightening sense washes over me, drenching my body in sweat.

It takes this sensation to root me in place—one singular, blaring moment of proof. I realize now how far gone I was. Without meaning to, without even controlling my arm, I reach for the amulet, for its strength. How often have I done that since I took it upon myself to protect the magic inside?

Slowly, the fog is lifted, and I am starting to see clearly, to feel true emotions—not just the ones the entity within thrust upon me as it took over my body, my mind, my sanity. It wanted me to fear my friends, to harness magic not meant for me. It didn't care that I was on the brink of demise, and the truth is its negative influence made me a monster.

My mind flashes to that dream—the one I had about Luna.

I was awash in the blood of the innocent, soaked from head to toe. The thick crimson essence covered every inch of my body. It seeped inside, absorbed through my skin, and rejuvenated my strength by stealing the spirit of another. I knew what was happening, but I didn't stop it.

I was rogue, and Luna was terrified of what she saw. She recognized the monster in me, the vile hint in my deviant gaze, and it muted her. I stole her voice, and I relished her fear. I wanted to kill her, so I did.

Even though I know that moment didn't happen, I hate myself. Because in the dream, I enjoyed what I did.

I blink away the memory, storing it in the very back of my mind. I close the door on it, shuttering the windows, turning off the light. The room I store this memory in is dark and dank, and everything I have done that fuels my regret is kept in there, hidden behind a locked, bloodred door.

Mentally, I throw away the key, telling myself I can never again relive this moment, because dreaming about being rogue is dangerous—too dangerous for a hybrid who once shared this mortal coil with an evil entity. It knows my sinister desires, my trembling fears, and it will use anything it can against me.

So I force these thoughts into exile, hidden behind a sealed door, but from the insidious depths of my mind, the light within that room still flickers. Because darkness as rich as this can never be truly extinguished.

I glance at the clock, desperate for yet another distraction. Though the seconds feel as though they pass by slowly—each tick another irrevocable strike against the nail in our coffin—the hours have flown by.

I try to be positive, but it's hard not to feel doomed, not to see downfall in everything we do. I spent my early years in combat, putting my life on the line every day for people who would have burned me at the stake if given the chance. I was cast out of my coven, banished from the only home I had ever known. And every day since I was ostracized, I have lost something.

So I focus on the clock, on the time, on the sound of the hammer hitting the head of the metaphorical nail that my life has become.

I frown and squint, as if that will allow my already-heightened vision to see more clearly.

The arms of the clock hands end in clear, decisive, daggered points, and I try to convince myself I am misreading their meaning. Because the little hand is pointed at the number eight, and the long hand is nearly touching the number six.

"It's half past eight," I say quietly.

Holland and Jeremiah glance up from where they are seated on the floor, a fresh stack of unread tomes towering before them. Jeremiah's brow furrows as he silently struggles to understand my meaning.

"It's almost nine," I whisper. "In the morning."

The others do not miss the horror in my tone.

It takes only a second for the fog to clear, for my words to pierce their minds, and I witness it all. I watch as the dread that consumes me overtakes my friends. We thought we had the upper hand, that the knowledge passed down through these grimoires would be enough to craft a spell strong enough to set everything right. I realize now that he saw this coming. We are merely puppets in this wicked game.

Jeremiah shouts for the others, his voice husky and low, and they trample into the room, joining us. The floorboards beneath my feet shake as they approach, rushing toward me in unison. When Malik is within arm's reach, he barrels past me. He forces the sheer curtain aside and stares out the bay window at the front of the house.

Not enough light shines through to even dimly illuminate the dark space.

Holland jumps to his feet, knocking into the floor lamp beside his tower of books, and it nearly collides with a nearby chair.

Jeremiah catches the lamp, his hand sliding up the metal rod, steadying the sole source of light in the room.

Their mouths are moving, but I hear nothing. Their voices, my heartbeat, even the blood rushing through the witch's veins, are silenced. But my mind screams. It is loud and vast, and it echoes all around me.

It's telling me to run.

I exit the parlor, entering the foyer, and throw open the front door. The handle smashes against the wall, and it caves. A deep gash is burrowed with the imprint of the knob, a stark reminder of the moment I lost my mind. Even now, as I stare at the damaged drywall, I feel it slipping away, and in the place of what should be sanity comes uncertainty.

I step outside, crossing the porch until I reach the stairs. They lead to a cobblestone path I can navigate from memory. I know every smooth surface, every ridge, every curve in the lawn, every crack in stone.

I descend the steps without looking down and cross the rocky pathway until I reach an open spot on the front lawn, where the sky is blocked by neither manor nor trees. The stars are gone, and I am staring at the sun.

# THREE

There is something particularly ominous about an eclipse—especially one as unnatural as this one.

Perhaps it feels like a sinister omen because of the lack of sunlight. After all, shadows are expert deceivers. If made of flesh and bone, they would thrive as tricksters, as prolific swindlers of even the most brilliant men.

Or maybe what chills my blood is that the bright light encircling the moon appears to be iridescent in color. It is not a burning red or a dim orange or even a subtle yellow. Instead, it looks purple where the sun rims the moon, but it morphs to a shimmery white as it emits outward. The eerie glow cascades down like a ring of violet fire, and somehow, it speaks to me, a siren call in the softest singsong voice.

The hunters are beside me, watching, waiting. They look to me with curious glances—almost as if they hear it too. But I know they don't, because this warning was meant for my ears alone. Like everything else in this godforsaken village, the truth of what is to come is my burden to bear.

The call of the moon is far too strong to break, so I don't return their gesture. I simply listen as she speaks to me. Her hum is sweet and pleading, a lullaby seeped in honey, but it is also tragic and bitter. Like the gloom of everlasting folklore, she hangs over us now, ghastly and sensational.

And as the moon swallows the sun, she tells me this world will soon burn.

My father is to blame. I don't need genius-level intellect to be certain of this. The idea to use magic to force an eclipse reeks of him. What better way is there for a child of the night to gain the upper hand than to cloak the world in eternal dusk?

But the magic used feels like my own. It beseeches me, touching the deepest parts of my soul. It feels warm and light and happy—as if I am to be congratulated for a job well done. I suppose if Papá is the reason for this phenomenon, it should feel like my magic courtesy of our familial link. Perhaps that tether will be his downfall.

"Your father has done this," Malik says, mirroring my thoughts.

His voice is cold and stern. It is a jarring contrast to the sizzling, welcoming magic that warms my heart.

"We have a much bigger problem than Ava's dad," Holland says. "The world has plummeted into darkness. Vampires everywhere have free rein. Humans won't survive another day if we don't stop this."

"We aren't prepared for this level of attack," Hikari says. "We can barely protect Darkhaven."

"We can't focus on the rest of the world right now," Malik says. "Keep it small. We must think only of here, now. If Ava's father is behind this, then he is the key to ending the eclipse. That in turn saves the world."

They look to me, and I wonder if they are expecting an objection. It would be natural to object, right? I should offer an alternate route that spares my father but leads to the same destination: saving the world and its mortal inhabitants.

But I don't object. I don't speak at all. Because they are

correct. Killing my father is the only way to set things right. To end this once and for all.

By tomorrow, my friends will ensure that Papá will regret returning to Darkhaven.

Malik opens his mouth to speak, but only a squeak of noise escapes his lips. He stops abruptly and frowns. His gaze flickers past me, and I focus on the deep burrow between his brows. His skin is creased in a harsh divot, the only telltale sign that he is much older than he appears. He is squinting—just like I do when disbelief and uncertainty cloud my vision, as if the action alone will offer the clarity we so desperately seek. But it never does.

I hear them approach. Their feet shuffle when they walk—a novice mistake. The toes of their shoes smack debris as they kick rocks and twigs. A scattering of dirt showers forward, spraying the ground several feet behind me. I don't need to see any of this to know what is happening. Because I hear it—from the sound of foot to brush, to their erratic heartbeats, to the deep inhalations of their overworked lungs. I hear it all.

But more than that, I can smell them. I can smell their fear. It is sour and stagnant, holding my attention much like my resentment. It is an all-consuming stench, serving as my blunt reminder that they are not allies.

Before I turn to face them, I take one long, slow breath. I hold it until my lungs burn, and then I release the trapped air.

Malik is watching me, his eyes fluttering between my wavering strength and the entourage approaching. I offer him a weak smile, one that I pray showcases my resolve and not my hesitancy.

Finally, I spin on my heels and face them.

The trees rustle when they emerge from the woods, and as

the last remaining witches of Darkhaven reveal themselves, I find myself lost to my thoughts. I think about things I shouldn't worry about right now, like the last time I saw my coven alive, the things we said, the hatred in our voices. I remember how hard I fought to bridge the gap between vampires and witches, to build an alliance that the world needed.

No one believed in my cause then, especially not our foe, yet they come to us now. The irony is strong with this one.

There is a small part of me that thrives on the idea of being spiteful and vindictive. Now that the world is enveloped by night, they need us. They *need* us. This is my chance for retribution, to hurt them as much as they hurt me. To reject them like they rejected me. To . . .

I blink and am back in reality. No longer living in my past, I see these witches for who they are: strangers. They are not from my coven. I know this. I know they can't be, because my coven was murdered. They're dead now. And with their demise, my chance at retribution was reduced to ash much like their seared flesh.

My gaze settles on the few witches I have seen before. One steps forward, and this time, I do not step back. I hold my ground, letting her approach me with a confidence that stuns me silent. Though she treads vampire territory under a darkened sky, she is not afraid.

I am torn between admiration and pity, because I understand her. If there is one tightrope I have teetered on since becoming a vampire, it is the fine line between strength and stupidity.

As she approaches me, the eclipse's eerie glow illuminates her tall, thin frame. She wears a floor-length black cotton dress that clings to her limbs as she struts forward, and her striking curls, still wild and frizzy, are billowing in the breeze. She is smiling at me, wide but sincere. Either she really, truly believes I am not a threat to her, or she has a few magical tricks up her sleeve. Either way, I must remain at a distance.

"Is this when you tell me you're happy I didn't take your advice and leave town?" I ask, halting her ascent.

I turn to see Malik frowning, and I shake my head. We haven't the time to discuss my earlier encounter with the witch—not when we are surrounded by the enemy, my sire is missing, and the world might literally end. Unfortunately, no one else seems to notice the silent conversation he and I are having.

"Wait..." Hikari says. "You two know each other?"

"I wouldn't phrase it that way," I say.

"How would you phrase it?"

"We met once, and she very bluntly told me to leave town and never return." I focus my attention solely on the witch now. "What was it you said?" I ask. "That I wasn't *welcome here*?" I use air quotes with my fingers to emphasize my point.

"You aren't safe here," she corrects. "I think it is quite clear that none of us are. Not anymore."

The witch glances up, and as her gaze is fixated on the eclipse looming overhead, she bares her neck to me. It is long and slender, like the rest of her bony frame, and her skin is milky white and supple and soft.

I am breathing heavier, heart pounding faster, and my gaze glosses over. In my mind's eye, all I can see is the throbbing vein in her untouched neck, and all I can hear is blood pulsating as it nourishes her mortal coil.

My tongue sticks to my dry lips when I lick them, and I swallow hard as a knot forms in my throat, threatening to choke the life from me.

Ever aware of his surroundings, my leader must notice my internal distress, because Malik loudly clears his throat. The sound reverberates all around me, rooting me in place, but still, I can't tear my eyes from her neck.

My hands are balled into fists at my sides because I do not trust my fingers. They are as eager as my blade, and her flesh is as inviting as bringing a hot knife to butter.

"What are you saying?" Malik asks. "Why do you believe we are no longer safe here?"

He steps forward, standing directly beside me. I notice his tall, bulky frame in my peripheral vision, but I cannot meet his gaze. He wraps his hand around my fist, blanketing my fingers with his own, and squeezes tightly, offering enough pressure to give me something to focus on that isn't my screaming hunger.

It works.

I catch my breath. It sounds as shaky as I feel. It escapes my lips in rolling bursts, and I am well aware that everyone around me can hear the fluctuating sound. The witch eyes me cautiously, but she does not move away.

"We want to help you," she says. "We want to work together to stop what is coming."

In response, Hikari and Holland speak in unison. Their words jumble together, creating resounding confusion as discouraging as the eclipse above.

"You want to work with vampires?" Hikari says.

"What do you think is coming?" Holland asks.

"Together? As in, side by side?" Hikari adds.

"I understand your hesitancy," the witch says. "But let me assure you, until this situation is resolved, there is no bad blood between us."

Hikari snorts, and I can practically taste her disbelief. I

can't blame her. I feel her anger. I too am maddened by their audacity.

How can they come to us now after everything that has happened? After everything they put us through? After months of forcing us to prove ourselves as allies only for them to deceive and destroy us? They thought we were the enemy, but the blood shed from fruitless feuds is on their hands. Will's blood. Amicia's blood. My friends were innocent. But these witches aren't.

They might not have aided my former coven at the time, but they aligned themselves with their goals, knowing what would happen, knowing the vampires could have used their help. They didn't choose us then, so I'm not convinced we should choose them now.

The witch is staring at Hikari. Her eyes are narrowed, mouth pursed. She doesn't approve of the outspoken vampire. Hikari, bold and defiant, goes against everything this witch stands for. There is a hierarchy to a coven, and the high priestess is not to be disobeyed or questioned. But unlike a vampire nest, which also embraces a hierarchy, there is no room for opposition.

When I was reborn as something different, Amicia took me in. She welcomed me into her home and treated me as one of her own, even though I was sired to another. I learned quickly that witches were never capable of such devotion, loyalty, or love. They care only about the big picture—so long as that vision fits their needs.

The witch stares at Hikari, and Hikari stares right back at her, never wavering. Malik is still standing beside me, so I jab my elbow into his arm. If he doesn't step in, I fear this contest will go on forever, and we definitely don't have the time to test egos.

"What exactly did you have in mind?" Malik asks.

The witch exhales sharply, tears her gaze away from Hikari's, and settles on me again, choosing to ignore my leader. I can't help but think her decision to do so is due to her pettiness. Hikari disrespected her, so she will disrespect Malik.

"Let's not get off on the wrong foot here," she begins. "We are aware of a vampire legion that has settled in Darkhaven."

I hold my breath at her words, waiting for the witch to mention my father's involvement in what will become the utter destruction of her beloved town. She now knows her entire belief system is built on a foundation of lies. She was convinced that witches are not capable of the dark deeds vampires commit, making the former better and worthy of life, but now she will have to admit her mistake. She will have to tell me a former witch is behind this dark reign.

"In fact, we have been tracking their movement as best we can for quite some time now—ever since your mother's coven was . . ."

She trails off, never quite summoning the words to accurately describe what a former witch did to his former coven.

"We hoped you could handle it—" she continues.

"You mean you hoped you wouldn't have to risk your lives," Jeremiah interrupts. "Just ours."

"Because we're expendable, right?" Hikari adds.

"Of course not," she says. "We hoped you would take care of it because they are your kind. You know how to best handle them. If witches were behind this, we would have stopped them ourselves."

"But a witch is behind this," Holland says.

The witch glances at me, and I think I see pity in her eyes.

Her gaze is murky, the depths as uncertain and dark as the sea that surrounds us, and I wonder if she might cry. But why does she mourn? Is she sorry for me, for my father, for my mother? Is she sorry a former witch is behind this, or is she sorry she knew him personally? Does she regret ever being friends with my family, wishing she knew then what we are capable of now?

"Yes, well, I am sure you can imagine why we think it is best to join forces," she says. "It will take both our magic and your innate strength to stop him."

Him. To stop . . . *him*. Much to my surprise, I sigh a breath of relief. Part of me wants her to admit the witches aren't as righteous and good as they claim to be, but a larger part doesn't want to keep talking about him. And if I'm being honest, I'm tired. I'm tired of apologizing for my past, and I'm tired of fighting for a future. Life isn't easy, but it shouldn't be this hard either.

"As I was saying," the witch continues, "it has become clear that we must intervene if we have any hope of survival."

"Why now?" I ask. "Why not intervene earlier?"

"I admit, it is a shame that we opted to wait," she says. "We truly did believe you could handle this on your own, but things have escalated."

The witch tilts her head back and points to the sky with her finger.

I look up as well, hoping to see even the slightest change. But it hasn't moved. The moon remains still, unyielding in its effort to govern what should be dominated by sunlight.

"Now that day is night, we are worried whatever he is planning will happen soon."

I nod.

"And unfortunately, this is only the beginning."

# FOUR

Witches and vampires enter the manor, skeptical and wary. The last time a coven entered our chambers, a line was drawn. Although it was etched by my own hand, I straddled that boundary, one foot firmly planted on both sides of this war, naïvely believing I could still bring my original goal to fruition. But instead of garnering peace, I cursed my coven that night and vowed to protect the black onyx crystal. I lost my grandmother, most of my nestmates, and my sanity.

Now, as witches shuffle through the foyer and into the parlor, there is no amulet, no bloodshed, no score to settle, but the fear from that fateful night remains.

At the other side of the room, the witches remain grouped together. They appear uneasy—arms crossed to cover their chests, bodies swaying methodically as their weight shifts from foot to foot. Beads of sweat scatter across their foreheads. The brackish stench of perspiration fills the room, but the odor is nothing compared to the sound of mortal bodies inhabiting an immortal domain.

Their heartbeats are deafening. In this enclosed space, blood swooshing through veins is as loud as waterfalls, and the hum of that relentless spill is enough to silence the room. My ears fall mute to all but one sound: the harmony of mortality— from the spark of nerves firing to the drag of elevated respiration.

Our guests summon—and hold—my undying admiration, because it takes the truly courageous to beckon aid from an enemy.

As my gaze flickers between the vampires and witches, I think about the countless gatherings we have had in this room. Convening as a group should feel familiar—dare I say, hopeful—because we have always executed our plans to our benefit. But this time is different. This time, we don't have the power to save ourselves. We need the witches as much as they need us.

"My idea is to harness the sun's energy, using its power over vampires in one burst of magic to kill the entire rogue army at once," Holland explains.

"What about the eclipse?" Hikari asks. "Can the spell still be done?"

"I think so," Holland says. "The sun is still there, even though it is hidden behind the moon."

"Even if it were night, we could still call upon the sun," I say. "It's always in the sky, even if it shines on another part of the world. Granted, the end result would be much weaker than if we completed the ritual during the day."

"True, but since we are targeting such a large group, we must cast the spell at the right time," Holland says. "We don't want to fail and find ourselves facing one furious rogue army."

"Perhaps the phenomenon will work in our favor," I suggest. "The moon is just as powerful as the sun, and the eclipse offers a unique power boost. Maybe we can use her magic too. Maybe it will be enough for our plan to work."

"That's my hope," Holland says. "Our original idea would only work if you guys take cover somewhere, because the spell will kill all vampires in the area, not just rogues. But maybe an eclipse will allow us to target specific vampires. Maybe the sun will kill the rogues, while the moon protects the hunters. It's a long shot, and perhaps not even possible, but I could try."

"And how do you expect to do this?" the leader of the witches asks. Her tone and frown assure me she has little confidence in our efforts.

"Well, I'm not sure," Holland says. "The ritual will require a great deal of magic, and I will likely need to summon the earthly elements, but—"

He is silenced by her raised hand.

"I am certain we can pool our resources and knowledge to create a spell and ritual that will harness the sun's energy," the witch says. "But what I am asking is how exactly do you plan to use this magic against only specific vampires?"

"Maybe target the soulless?" I ask.

"The soulless?" she repeats.

"This may come as a shock to you, but not all vampires are the same," I say. "You and I fight for the same cause. The creatures you fear are rogue vampires. They're evil, soulless fiends that live exclusively on the blood of the innocent. We're nothing like them. We fight to protect Darkhaven and the humans who live here."

"Yet we are in the very place where your grandmother was killed, are we not?" she says. "How many witches lost their lives here? And of those, how many deaths were at the hands of the vampires you deem good?"

"You aren't the only ones who lost someone that day," Jeremiah says, seething.

I understand his pain and the loss he feels for his sire. Not a second passes when I don't think about Jasik, but we need to think clearly, to put our emotions aside if we are to fix this.

If we rip each other down now, no one will be here to build us back up. Our friends—and all of Darkhaven, for that matter—are counting on us.

"The witches of Darkhaven have brought us nothing but death, pain, and war—even while we risk our necks to save yours," Malik says. "Is it not hypocritical of you to label us evil while your kind murders without consequence?"

"We define murder as killing barbarously," she says. "And there is nothing savagely cruel, uncivilized, or harsh about ridding this mortal plane of immortal creatures, especially ones that survive on human bloodshed."

"You have a lot of nerve, lady," Jeremiah says. "How dare you enter our home and—"

"Enough!" I shout.

My frustration gets the best of me, unraveling a chain of events the others cannot ignore. And with my anger, something changes. It's like time ceases altogether, and at its standstill, I feel utterly alone.

My fury causes the blood in my veins to turn icy, and the air becomes crisp and cool. With my hands clenched into fists at my sides, the house begins to shake. Floorboards splinter as a shock wave spreads from the soles of my feet.

"We don't have time for this," I hiss. "For those who have forgotten, our mutual enemy has our amulet and our friend. He has stolen the sun, and he has an army of monsters far stronger than any of us. If we can't set aside our differences for this one cause, then we might as well kill each other right now. Because we don't deserve the gifts we have been given."

"You're right," the witch says. "I'm sorry. This isn't the time to discuss past events."

"I shouldn't have to remind any of you that this town is

counting on us to get our shit together," I say. "So if you have nothing productive to add, shut up. If you think of something useful, speak. It's that simple."

The room falls silent.

And then Holland looks up. "Unfortunately, I'm afraid the spell will be incredibly complicated. We will need a full coven's magic, timely words, elemental magic, and something to contain the power of the sun, and without the amulet—"

"We are willing to aid you in this," the witch says. "As Ava so aptly mentioned, we fight the same cause. If your intent is to eliminate the vampire army, then you have our full support."

"Well, that checks off one item on the list," Holland says. "But like I said, we need more than just a coven's power."

"Two," I say. "Two items are checked off. We still have the Orb of Helios. It's strong enough to channel the power of the sun."

"Yes, right," Holland says.

"The Orb of Helios?" the witch says. "You have one?"

"Yes," Holland says.

He eyes the small brown box. It rests atop a stack of tomes, and he grabs it, pulling it close. He holds it protectively, guarding it against a possible heist. If the witches notice his demeanor, they say nothing.

"How?" the witch asks. "They are quite rare. Even I haven't seen one before."

"Does that really matter?" I ask, not bothering to hide my annoyance. "The point is, we have one, and we can use that to harness the sun's power."

"Have you an Orb of Selene?" the witch asks, and I don't miss her snooty tone. "If you do, we could use that to harness the moon's power. Perhaps together—"

"We don't," Holland says. "We were lucky enough to get our hands on the Orb of Helios."

"Well, we do," she says, smiling widely.

"You have an Orb of Selene?" Holland asks in disbelief.

Rather than respond, she simply offers a coy smile. She looks at me momentarily, but I can't read her eyes.

"There's no way this is happenstance," Holland says, voice giddy.

His abrupt change in tune catches my attention. Reluctantly, I tear my vision from the woman. I make a mental note to figure out her true intentions once and for all—after we have a plan, that is.

"I mean, what are the odds that the only witches willing to help us have the one relic we need to succeed?" Holland continues.

"Perhaps luck is on our side," Jeremiah says.

Like the rest of us, he's trying to remain hopeful, but no one matches Holland's level of excitement at this point.

"Or maybe it's more than that," Hikari says. "Don't you think the timing is suspicious? This wouldn't be the first time we trusted the wrong people. Witches have never been kind to us."

"Guys, with this orb, we might actually win this thing!" Holland says. "We have to focus on that right now."

"Let's not get ahead of ourselves," the witch says. "We may have both orbs, but we still need to craft a spell to summon the sun's power."

The witch doesn't comment on our lingering distrust. I suppose she doesn't have to. There isn't much she can say to ease our nerves. Both are correct. The timing is suspicious, but with their help and both orbs, we can beat the rogues. When my father is gone once and for all, we'll discover the witches' true motives. Until then, we take on one battle at a time.

"The Orb of Helios should do most of the work," Holland counters. "In fact, I think we can tweak the average sun spell in our favor."

"How does that help us?" Malik asks. "I was under the assumption that a spell of this magnitude doesn't exist."

"The ritual we will perform hasn't been done before, but using the sun's strength to boost spells is common practice," I say. "In fact, once we complete the ritual, the sun's power should naturally flow into the Orb of Helios. It was made to contain that magic. The hard part will be removing it from the orb and using it to kill the rogues."

"I'm less concerned with the possibility of actually making this work and more concerned with finding a way to keep you guys alive," Holland says. "I'm still not sure how to write a sun spell that will distinguish rogues from hunters."

"Isn't that what the Orb of Selene is for?" Hikari asks.

"Theoretically, yes," Holland says, his earlier excitement dwindling.

"Moon magic does exist," I say. "And we can use it to our advantage. After all, we walk in moonlight every day, so the magic you need is there. You just need to tap into it. It should transfer to the Selene as easily as sun magic flows into the Helios."

"The issue is directing moon magic to just you and sun magic to just them. This is going to get complicated . . ." Holland sighs heavily. He runs a hand through his hair, scratching at his scalp as his eyes gloss over.

He doubts his ability, his power, and I don't blame him. We're asking him to do what he thinks is impossible. Best case scenario, he makes it work and we save the day. Worst case scenario, he watches his friends and boyfriend die with the rest of the rogue army. Having just lost my coven to fire, I understand his hesitation.

"What if…"

As I fall silent, the room disappears, and I lose myself in my thoughts. My mind is swirling with the birth of an idea—one that works in theory but perhaps not in reality.

"Ava?" Malik says. "What is it?"

"The Orb of Selene is made of moonstone," I say. "It's one of the only crystals strong enough to harness the moon's energy. Hence the name."

"That's correct," the witch says. "And the Orb of Helios is made of sunstone. What of it?"

"We are using the Orb of Helios to harness the sun's power," I say as I continue to work through my mental roadblocks. "Our hope is to somehow tap into the orb and basically shower the area in sunlight."

"Right…" Holland says. His brow furrows as he tries to connect the dots.

"So we are redirecting that flow of magic," I say. "We're taking it from the orb and basically bursting it all around us so that it consumes the rogue vampires. It'll be like forcing a sunrise."

"That's the plan," Holland says. "But that's also the issue. You guys will be there too. You'll die with them unless we find a way to shield you."

"Exactly. We need to be shielded," I say. "What if we do the same thing with the Orb of Selene? What if we redirect the moon magic, but in a more specified manner? If it works, the moonlight will envelop us, right? That might be enough to offset the power of the sun."

"How would we do that?" Malik asks.

"Is it even possible to shield us and not them?" Hikari adds.

"We use moonstone amulets," I say. "We will each wear one. That should direct the moon magic to our specific persons."

"Hypothetically speaking, that could work," Holland says.

He cradles his chin in his hand and rubs the scruff that has grown after days of neglect. Like the others, the stress of what we have endured shows in the dark circles under his eyes.

"But how?" Jeremiah asks. "And why? How would it keep us safe? Why would that work?"

"Yeah, let's keep in mind we don't have the best track record with amulets," Hikari says pointedly.

"The moonstone would attract the moon magic that we release from the orb," Holland says. "Basically, anyone wearing the amulet would be cast in moonlight, and when the sun's energy is released, you shouldn't be harmed."

"Shouldn't?" Hikari repeats.

"It's not a perfect plan," Holland says. "But this isn't a perfect situation. This is probably the best chance we have at making this work."

"*Probably?* These are the kinds of words I don't like hearing when we're already seriously outnumbered."

"Hikari," Malik says, voice stern.

"I know you're scared," Holland says. "I am too, but I think this will work. I mean . . . this *will* work."

"It will. It has to," I say. "We'll strengthen the amulets with everything we have—the power of the eclipse, elemental magic, coven magic. Maybe we can even find a way to use my hybrid strength to seal the spell. Whatever it takes to make the moon spell and our amulets stronger than the sun."

"It might take your life," Hikari says. "All of our lives. If this doesn't work—"

"If we don't try," I say, "we're dead anyway."

I sit on the front porch landing, legs draped over the steps beneath me. Staring into the dark distance, I take several deep breaths, letting the morning air wash over me. The last time I was outside during daylight hours, I was mortal.

Even though the sun is hidden by the moon, I still feel its presence. It's an eerie sensation that is nothing like the warm embrace I remember. My body knows it's supposed to be daytime hours, and my instincts are telling me to run. I fight the urge and rub the chill from my arms.

I squeeze my eyes shut as my stomach grumbles. Our refrigerator is nearly empty. Only a few blood bags remain. Mentally, I calculate what this means. Even if we share our supply, taking a few sips each, we will quickly grow weak, and weakness means we will be susceptible to an attack. Rogues are naturally stronger opponents, so we need to feed properly if we plan to win this war once and for all.

I try to distract myself by thinking of Jasik, but that only makes me think of my father. And thinking of him just makes me angry. He has both the amulet and my sire, and right now, he's probably laughing.

He thinks he's won. He thinks I have no choice but to surrender to him. If I believed he would actually release Jasik, I would, but I know he won't. Waving the white flag will only result in our capture and his win.

Malik emerges from the tree line and strides toward me. He has just finished his sweep, and next, Jeremiah will take over. Calculated patrolling on a rotating shift is the only way we know how to protect the manor, and the witches inside are relying on us to keep them safe.

"How is it going in there?" Malik asks.

His eyes flicker between my own and the bay window behind me. Just beyond that window is the parlor, where the witches have gathered to discuss our futures. The distinct cackle of too many people speaking at the same time wafts closer.

They're arguing. Again.

I shake my head and exhale sharply. "It's been like that since you left. They agree on the plan but not much else."

Malik nods and sits beside me. His leg brushes against mine, and shock waves shoot through my limbs. He stiffens beside me, as though he feels the connection too, but he says nothing.

"We won't accomplish much with them fighting like this," I say.

"It's difficult to let someone else be the leader when that's all you've ever known."

"Are you talking about the witches . . . or you?"

He grins, but it fades quickly. The more time I spend with Malik, the easier it becomes to read him. I can barely remember that emotionless vampire who trained me how to be undead.

"Holland has been a solitary witch for a long time," Malik says. "I imagine it's difficult for him to now work as a team, and I'm sure the others aren't eager to take orders from him . . . or from us. They all just need some time."

"We don't have time to waste. My father will come for us, and we must be ready."

"Let me worry about your father. Just focus on your breathing. It'll help calm your nerves."

"I'm not sure I can function properly if I'm not stressing about something," I say, chuckling.

This time, he doesn't hold back his smile. His smirk is wide and true, and his eyes flash to mine. He looks at me lovingly, protectively—the way a brother might look at his younger sister. He doesn't speak about it, but I know he feels responsible for me, for keeping me safe. I know arguing that I can take care of myself would be pointless.

"Have you considered what you will do when you see your father?"

"I know what I will do," I say. "I'll do what I have to."

"Ava…"

Malik sighs heavily, shaking his head as he averts his eyes. He fingers the fabric of his jeans where it is bunched at his knees, letting the silence linger between us. I wait for him to finish.

"I don't envy any man—or woman—who has to do the unthinkable," Malik says. "What we're asking of you—to kill your own father—isn't okay. You shouldn't be in this situation. It shouldn't be your responsibility to take his life."

"You're right. I shouldn't be in this situation, but I am. And that's his fault. Now, I have to do what needs to be done."

"I'm only suggesting—"

"He's evil."

"He is. But it doesn't have to be you. You don't need to be the one who kills him."

"There is no one else."

He frowns and turns toward me. His eyes pierce mine, and I see the pain in them. But I don't know what hurts him more—that I feel alone in this or that I won't lean on him the way I have leaned on his brother.

"I will do this for you," he whispers.

"Are you only offering because you want to kill him?"

"I want to save you."

"Save me?" I repeat, voice shaky.

"Killing someone you love stains your soul. It's something you can never wash away. It'll keep you awake at night, and even though you will try to convince yourself that you were right, that you did what must be done, that they were evil and you did what you did to save innocents, you will still hate yourself for what you did. You will carry that hate and that anger with you for the rest of your life, Ava. Eternity is a long time to live in that darkness."

His hands are balled into white-knuckled fists and resting on his thighs. His eyes are narrowed, lips pursed, brow creased. The moment I place my hand atop his, the tension eases. I see it wash over him as he shakes it away, blinking back to reality. I don't know what nightmare he was just reliving, but I want to protect him from it. I don't want him to ever go there again.

"You're a good man, Malik," I whisper.

He licks his lips and exhales slowly. This time, he doesn't look at me when he speaks.

"I haven't always been," he says. "And that is my burden to bear. But you have a long future ahead of you. You don't need to do this."

"But it should be me."

"Why? Because you feel responsible? You were a child when they came for your family. There was nothing you could have done. It's time you stop blaming yourself for his death."

"If only it were that easy . . ."

"Then forgive yourself," he says. "If you can't see that it wasn't your fault, that his attack had nothing to do with you, at least forgive yourself for what happened."

"I'll forgive myself when it's over."

# FIVE

I tense as the witch approaches from behind. The skin at the back of my neck prickles, and a soft breeze—a slight shift in the air as she invades my space—alerts me to her nearness.

Even as she halts, my body continues its involuntary reaction to her presence. My breath catches in my lungs as I clench my jaw shut tightly, and I ball my hands into fists at my lap. Malik, forever eerily observant, must notice the abrupt demeanor change, because he places a hand over mine. For one blissful second, I forget that she's here.

But then she's there again, treading closer, and all at once, she consumes me. Her breath, deep and raspy, sounds like ocean waves. Her heart screams, a desperate echo from its desolate depths. Her blood swooshes like a river . . . like a long, swift riptide that pulls me down into those cool murky waters.

I lick my lips.

As her scent washes over me, I hum softly and close my eyes. She is still several feet behind me, but I feel her warmth as though her body is thrust against mine. It radiates from her thin form, piercing my own, shredding my innards until nothing remains but my empty, hollow, hungry gut.

I'm starving . . .

The realization grounds me, silencing my own overworked heart. The desire to feed, to relish in the strength only a full belly provides, makes my fangs throb.

This is what it feels like when a vampire forgoes sustenance. I am so frantic to silence the agony that I consider drinking my own.

Also, it doesn't help that I despise this woman. My hatred for the witches burrows deep. Hungry and angry are never a good combination.

"You should go inside," Malik orders, voice stern.

I open my eyes. He is standing now, teetering on the steps as he faces the witch behind me. I don't even remember when he let go of my hand.

"I need to speak with Ava," the woman says.

Shakily, I stand and face her. My grip on the handrail makes the wood splinter.

With exhaustion settling over the entire manor, everyone inside is succumbing to the stress of this night. Even the witch feels it. Her wrinkles are more pronounced, and the dark divots beneath her eye sockets mock my perfect porcelain skin.

That's the danger of a mortal befriending a vampire. She has no idea how tired I am, how ornery, how hungry, how close I am to crossing that line. As an immortal, blood controls all that I do, and without it, all I can think about is where to find another source.

"You can speak later," Malik says. "After we've fed."

She sucks in a sharp breath. The wood creaks beneath her weight as she shifts uncomfortably from foot to foot. She winces at his words, face cringing into an unattractive frown.

I know the look well. When I was alive, I felt that same disgust. The thought of a feeding vampire makes her squirm. She believes us to be unnatural, but I've found we're simply another stop in the circle of life. We have a purpose, even if the witches of Darkhaven refuse to see it.

"I'm not leaving," she says. Her stubbornness just may be her greatest flaw. She'll take it to her grave.

Malik's eyes narrow, and the tiny muscles in his jaw twitch from annoyance. As he considers his options, he grinds his teeth and exhales so loudly it's all I can hear.

He doesn't speak right away. His irises glaze over, a sight I have seen many times before. He is considering his options. He can't simply force her inside. The others won't take too kindly to that, and we need them right now. We can't rescue Jasik or stop my father without their magic. But submitting to her isn't in his nature. He's a leader, not a follower.

He glances at me.

"I think we have one blood bag left," Malik says. "I'll bring it to you."

I nod. I hate the thought of taking our last form of sustenance, but I'm too hungry to turn down an easy meal. The others will need to hunt, scouring the woods for animal prey. Maybe they'll get lucky and find several grazing deer.

Malik never breaks eye contact with the witch as he passes. When he enters the foyer, he leaves the front door open. Following his silhouette, I watch as he disappears into the darkness at the back of the house. And all at once, she and I are alone.

"Is he always that tense?" she asks.

I shrug, gaze still glued to the shadows. The answer is yes. Malik is the most intense vampire I have ever met. He carries himself differently than the others. His presence screams of a man burned and burdened.

"You'll get used to it," I say.

"I should hope not."

I snort and roll my eyes.

"And you wonder why we keep you at a distance?" I ask, finally meeting her eyes. "You don't seem keen to actually work with us."

"I'll be honest, Ava. If this wasn't your nest, I don't know that I would have showed up here. I don't like the idea of aiding vampires. There is a reason the species have lived separately all these years. It's what works."

"But does it?" I ask. "Look at what's happened. Look at all we've lost. And now, we're on the cusp of exposure. Dealing with humans as a threat is something neither of us are prepared for."

Malik clears his throat. He tosses a lone blood bag to me from where he stands in the doorway, never stepping foot on the porch. The blood bag now airborne, Malik crosses his arms over his chest and eyes the witch cautiously. She stares back, and an epic, silent battle of wills ensues.

I ignore them both because I can't take my eyes off the contents now swirling in my hands. It is cold, the liquid a dark crimson color, thick and rich. Just the sight makes my mouth water.

My fangs lengthen ever so slightly, a drop barely noticeable by human eyes. But I sense the difference. It is the difference between a smile and a hiss, between seductively dragging my teeth against my bottom lip and tearing through flesh. It is the difference between predator and prey.

I rip open the bag and greedily swallow its contents. Blood coats my tongue, my throat, spilling into my stomach. Immediately, I am soothed. No longer crazed by irritability and insanity, I moan as I lick my lips, gaze glued to the empty bag.

When I glance back up, Malik is backing away. He disappears inside.

"Why did you want to speak with me?" I ask.

The witch is focused on the blood bag in my hand, so I shove it in my pocket. I ascend the steps and lean against the railing at the height of the stairs. I am eye-to-eye with the witch now, waiting in silence for her to answer my question.

"I—I wanted to know what your plans are . . . after."

I am silent as I think about her words. Ironically, as a creature with a vast sea of time before me, I don't think about the future much. I spend too much of my time just hoping to survive the next day. But now that we know my father has orchestrated everything that's happened since my transition, it's safe to assume things will calm down once he's gone. I just might have a future after all.

Then I remember her warning the day she saw me outside the magic shop.

"You still think I need to leave Darkhaven?" I ask. "Isn't this the reason it's unsafe here? Because of the rogues?"

She shakes her head. "I'm not so sure. Things are changing in Darkhaven. Humans are becoming suspicious. They're bringing in outsiders."

"The fire investigator," I say softly.

"He's here to deal with what happened. It's only a matter of time before he discovers the truth."

"He came with family. He intends to stay here. For good."

She frowns. "How do you know that?"

"I was there the day you brought flowers to my mother after the fire," I say, deciding to be honest. "You left the bundle on what remained of our front stoop. I saw him stop you."

She blinks several times at the realization that I was watching her, stalking from the shadows. She had no idea that I was there.

"Why were you watching me?"

"I wasn't there for you. I was there . . . to see."

I don't elaborate because I don't think I need to. Because she nods. She understands. She sniffles and swipes a finger at her nose.

"Your mother was a dear friend," she says.

"Then why don't I know you? I don't even know your name. You want me to trust you, to believe you, but how can I? I don't know anything about you."

"I suppose you wouldn't remember me. After your father died, your mother . . . changed. She once believed in combining the separate covens and forming a high council of elders. She thought we could keep the town safer by working toward a similar goal."

"What happened?" I ask.

"Your father. His murder changed her. She became—"

"Bitter. Angry. Hateful."

The witch nods. "She wasn't interested in working together anymore. She was only interested in killing, in avenging his death by eliminating as many vampires as possible. The last time you saw me was at your father's funeral," she adds.

"I don't remember . . ."

"I suppose you wouldn't. You were young, and so was I. Not all of us will appear seventeen forever."

I chuckle, amazed that the witch joked about my being a vampire. I truly didn't believe she had it in her to make light of vampirism.

"You called me Sunshine," she said. "My hair was a wavy bright blond back then, and I always tucked an orange flower above my ear. I think it reminded you of the sun."

"What should I call you now?" I ask. "Or do you still go by Sunshine?"

She smiles brightly, blindingly, almost like the sun.

"No, sadly, no one else has ever called me that," she says. "You can call me Aurelia."

At the sound of her name, I am suddenly a child again.

I am huddled against my bedroom door, ear pressed firmly against the wood. I am eavesdropping on my mother's phone call. Her words are muffled by distance, but I can make out a few here and there. Still, that isn't enough for my eager mind, so I sneak into the hallway and crouch at the top landing. She is angry, and even though I have now long since forgotten most of what she was saying, I do remember one word.

*Aurelia.*

She was speaking to the witch, and Mamá wasn't happy.

"You said you didn't speak with my mother after my father's funeral, but I remember her talking to you," I say. "I heard her on the phone."

"Well, in all fairness, I said I didn't see you after your father's funeral. But I most certainly tried to remain friends with your mother. I worried about her, about you. I just didn't want her to feel like she was alone."

"But she did. I think she was very lonely. She always believed my father would come home. She feared change so much. She wouldn't even paint our house for fear that doing so would mean he couldn't recognize the one he called home."

"Grief changes people, Ava. And the guilt never goes away."

I turn away from the witch and stare into the distance. The world, which should be illuminated by the sun, is still cast in shadows, but I find comfort as darkness reigns—especially right now, when Aurelia's words leave me raw.

I can't let her see how she affects me.

But she's right. My guilt consumes me, and much like my grief, it lingers like a noose, muffling my cries. I fear it will never loosen, that I will never catch my breath.

When I look at my reflection, I barely recognize the girl staring back at me. It's almost as if the vampire is nothing like the mortal I used to be. I was strong, fearless. Now, I just feel weak, with days tied together by endless mistakes.

As a witch, I was willing to lay down my life for our cause. I believed, wholeheartedly, in what I was taught, in what the witches convinced me was true. I engaged in battle recklessly, never questioning if my actions were justified.

Even if I don't recognize myself anymore, I know that inherent naïvety is the reason we're in this mess. It's why Jasik was abducted and the amulet was stolen, and even though I'll never say the words aloud, part of me wishes I still had the black onyx crystal. Its power could make everything right again, but in harnessing its magic, I would lose myself . . . again.

Am I willing to make that trade?

Am I still that girl who would lay down her life for those she loves?

# SIX

Aurelia and I have been sitting in silence for several minutes now, both lost to our own inner turmoil. And in that time, the commotion inside has reached ear-piercing—and rogue-alerting—levels.

I hoped I could ignore them, that I could lose myself to my own demons and let the others work out their problems without my intervention. I guess I was wrong.

With a groan of frustration, I stand, taking what little enjoyment I can in the dramatics of stomping my boots against the wooden steps. Aurelia tramples beside me, nearly tripping over her own feet as she fails to keep up with my speed.

I enter the foyer and stop when I come face-to-face with the others. Standing in the doorway of the parlor, I blink several times as I take in the scene. I feel like the mother of teenagers, and like any good mother, I ready myself for a battle of wills and wits.

"What the hell is going on?" I shout, forgoing pleasantries.

The scene before me is nothing like the room I left. The energy has completely warped. Only an hour ago, we had a plan in motion. Holland was giddy with joy, with hope at the prospect of winning. All they had to do was write the damn spell. Summon the sun, use the orbs, kill some rogues, call it a day. That was the plan, right? What could have possibly

50

happened since then to make everyone fight . . . *again*?

The room silences, and I can only assume it's my death-dagger stare that leaves them motionless.

Malik is across the room, leaning against the fireplace with his arms crossed over his chest. He is staring at the ground, looking utterly defeated. My heart softens at the sight of him. This isn't what he signed up for when he agreed to lead this group of misfits.

"What's the problem?" I ask. "Were we not all in agreement on what we were going to do? Did I just imagine the part when we said we would create a sun spell and use the orbs?"

"We've encountered a . . . wrinkle," Holland says.

He is standing beside Jeremiah, who looks as annoyed as I feel. The other witches are standing as well, almost completely encircling the hunters. The room feels . . . tense, the vibe completely different from what I felt when I left them to get some air. I'm not sure what happened in the time it took for me to come back, but we don't have time for this. Jasik doesn't have time for this.

"What kind of wrinkle?" I ask, voice stern.

I am trying hard to control my budding frustration, but I can't seem to keep the attitude out of my tone. I'm at the end of my rope, and I'm about ready to jump in without them. They don't want that. I don't want that. Because despite having the best of intentions, I always seem to mess things up when I run off half-cocked. We need to be smart if we want to win this, and spending what little time we have left arguing isn't smart. In fact, we're doing what my father is hoping we're doing: wasting time.

I think about Holland's vague explanation for the all-out

war happening between them and us.

A wrinkle.

*We've encountered a wrinkle.*

"Please, please, please, don't tell me you can't do the sun spell."

"I thought it was agreed that I would be the vessel," Holland says. "But they seem to think I'm just a helper at this shindig. That's not how it will go down."

He glances from me to the witches, glaring when he meets their eyes. His disdain is evident. Like the others, he's just not used to working with the opposite side. We used to be on our own—vampires, witches, humans. Now we're working together against a common enemy: rogue vampires. There are bound to be mishaps, but if we stop communicating, we'll never come up with a plan that will succeed.

"What do you mean?" I ask.

"I mean, I am not a backseat driver!" Holland yells. His voice cracks. He crosses his arms over his chest in what I can only define as utter frustration.

"Holland, I don't understand what you're saying."

I keep my voice calm, my temperament cool, even though every fiber of my body wants to shake some sense into the witch. What is he even talking about? Instead of being productive and finding a way to save Jasik, he's ranting about shindigs and backseat drivers. He's making no sense.

"Someone has to summon the sun's power," Holland says. "That person is the vessel."

Yes, we established this the last time we gathered to talk logistics ... But I don't say this out loud. I opt for something less antagonistic. It seems like the healthier approach.

"Okay ... And?"

"And that person should be me," Holland says. "I need to be the vessel."

"And you have an issue with that?" I ask, turning to face Aurelia.

I've blindly followed several different leaders in my young life—from my grandmother to my mother to Amicia to Malik—and despite different origins, they all carry the same burden. As the leader, they speak for those who follow them.

A flash of confusion crosses Aurelia's face, but her pinched features distort her natural beauty only for a second. She may have been as taken aback as I was by this abrupt change in plans, but now, she hides her emotions well. Her confusion is gone, replaced by an icy stare.

Aurelia briefly glances at the others before her gaze settles back on me. She clears her throat.

"Yes, it makes sense that we be the vessel," she says.

"Why?"

"Because we are a coven. We can work as a collective being. Holland is a solitary practitioner. He may be powerful, but he is no match for our pooled strength."

"Ava..." Holland says, trailing off.

He and I lock gazes, and he shakes his head slowly. His jaw is clenched tightly, and his stare—cold and stern—makes me shiver. I understand his apprehension, his fear. If we hand over control to the witches, who is to say they won't use the sun's power against us too? Our goal is to kill rogue vampires. Witches have always intended to annihilate all immortals. They deem us unnatural despite the fact that we've only wanted peace. Because of this, Holland fears for our safety, for Jeremiah's safety.

"No," I say. "Holland will be the vessel."

He sighs. It's a loud, harsh burst of relief that recharges the room's already-chaotic energy. He smiles at me, silently thanking me with his eyes, but I didn't make this decision for him. I made it for all of us. As much as we hope to trust these witches, we can't go blindly into this fight. They're not our friends, and treating them like they are will end up with some of us dead. I can't take that risk.

"Ava, don't be rash," Aurelia says. "Think about this. We have a greater chance of success if we control the magic. A coven is more powerful than one witch. It's really quite simple math."

"I understand your argument, Aurelia," I say, grinding my teeth at her persistence. "It's your intentions that are unclear, and unfortunately, we haven't the time to garner trust. Holland will be the vessel."

"You're being foolish!" Aurelia shouts. "We have no hidden agenda. There are no conspiracies here."

"If you're worried about the safety of your coven, create an infallible ritual." This time, I don't bother to hide my annoyance. I let it coat my words in a thick drawl like some heavy accent. I've made up my mind, and nothing she has to say will change it.

Still, she doesn't take the hint that this discussion is over.

"You know magic doesn't work that way. There are no guarantees. Even if we write a perfect spell, there is still a chance of it not working. At least with a collective power source, we can increase our odds."

"It's really quite simple," I say, mirroring her words from earlier. "If you're as powerful as you say you are, then you can find a way to make this work with Holland as the vessel."

"This way of thinking will get us all killed!" she hisses.

"I said *no!*" As I shout, I throw out my arms, but what was meant as a display of melodramatic finality turns into something far more eerie.

The room falls silent, gazes glued to my movements. Only the crackling air, which is rapidly overheating with such fever I fear we will all combust, separates them from me.

I stare in disbelief at my outstretched arms. I am surrounded by magic, by *my* magic. My body is fiery hot, and as this raw, untapped power seeps from every pore, it sizzles against my skin. I realize my own tingling flesh is the crackling sound we hear, and it bounces off the walls like some sick echo chamber.

My chest heaves as I struggle to steady my breathing, and I am slick with sweat. I feel it drip from my temples down to the curvature of my jaw before it splashes onto my chest. Some even pools on the hardwood. I am still looking down, still staring in disbelief, eyes nearly parallel with the floor. I just can't believe what I am seeing.

I am coated in an iridescent glow, and with each passing second, as the power inside me intensifies, the shimmer surrounding my body blazes brighter.

It's been so long since I last summoned the witch within, I almost forgot what it felt like to be completely consumed by my magic. It's a rush. It feels like all my senses are rapid firing at once. I can hear colors. I can taste sounds. It's so strong, I can barely breathe, barely stand upright, yet I still feel so totally free, so at ease.

The witch's energy courses through my veins, strengthening the very bones of my being. As we unite, I am rejuvenated with each breath I take. I become stronger as each second passes.

It took nearly killing my friends and finally, bitterly releasing a cursed amulet to realize how deeply that evil entity entombed me. Now, it has taken the loss of my sire and the looming threat of a town annihilation to realize that I have relied on the vampire for too long. I forgot what the world felt like for someone without undead heightened senses, without great speed and endurance, without the desire for bloodshed. Since my transition, I've lost a piece of her every day, and as the vampire grew stronger, as I slowly accepted my fate as a daughter of moonlight, I silenced the witch. I smothered her needs.

I. Am. A. Hybrid.

I repeat this sentiment again and again, as the magic swirling inside my body finally reaches my mind, smashing through the barrier that separated my two halves. As I finally accept them both, I become whole, and I feel . . . different.

I am a hybrid—part vampire, part witch. I stand squarely between two worlds, never fully embracing either. I forget this fact too easily and too often. I need both the witch and the vampire to feel complete, to feel truly powerful.

When I handed Sofía the crystal, I rid myself of the evil contained within it, but I never released my own darkness. It still imprisoned me. But as a girl just trying to do what's right, a girl standing before a coven I do not know and do not trust, I didn't use my vampire strength to convince them that our way is better. I summoned the witch. I reminded them that I too come from greatness, that we too can handle such powerful magic.

I wasn't just born from blood. I was born from power.

I needed to remind them of that.

I stand upright. Arms dangling at my sides, I clench my

fists, digging my nails into the palms of my hands. I've done this very stance more times than I can count. It grounds me and gives me the confidence boost I so desperately need in times like this.

My magic still lingers, but that burst of energy is slowly dissipating. Still, I can't continue to relish in the feeling anymore. I can't wait any longer. We've already wasted too much time. Someone will bear the cost of our mistakes tonight, and I can only hope that individual isn't someone we love.

I steady myself for a few breaths before speaking. I let oxygen fill my lungs until they stretch so much it hurts, and then I exhale long and slow. Each time I do this, I am reminded why we are here. It makes me angry, but more importantly, it makes me sad.

"Vampires and witches have been around since the dawn of time," I say. "And for the better part of hundreds of thousands of years, all we've managed to do is kill each other. While we have been at war, humans have made their mark in this world. They have claimed it as their own, and all we can do is watch while wearing masks. We must hide behind the illusion of normality just for a chance to survive. Because we all fear the day they find out.

"Instead of working together to stop the bloodshed and keep our existence a secret, we just keep hurting each other. We've lost too many because of a fruitless war. In the last few months alone, we've lost entire covens. We fight over the mundane, and even though we know what we're arguing about is trivial, we continue. We're too hateful and too dense to see that we want the same thing."

There is movement now. No longer staring in silence, jaws slack in disbelief, they move, weight shifting from foot to foot.

Almost in unison, they begin this shuffle, swaying from side to side. They're uneasy being called out, but that discomfort only fuels me more. I have no plans to stop.

"How many times have I made this speech? How many times have I asked for peace only to be met with animosity? We could have saved those lost too early, but it's too late now. They're dead, and more will join them. If we can't stop arguing and start listening, then death to all is inevitable.

"And make no mistake. We will all die in this battle. All of us. Every single being in this room, vampire and witch, will die. Tonight. We have absolutely no chance against an army of rogue vampires. They are stronger. They are faster. They are better in almost every way. They are more savage than any beast you have ever fought, and the reason they are such incredible and unstoppable killing machines is because they are driven by just one thing: blood. They do not care about life or death or winning or losing. They don't care about exposure. They have a singular focus, and they will stop at nothing to get it. The only way we can beat such brute force is if we work together. If we align ourselves in this one cause, we can outsmart them. Because let's face it—that's all we have. Brains. We have brains. They have brute. That's as basic as I can make this for you.

"And the really messed-up part is that we don't have to die tonight. We can win this if we work together. But you're all too stubborn to put your prejudices aside. You have spent your entire lives fighting these battles. Aren't you tired of it? Aren't you sick of waking up and wondering if today's the day your enemy will finally best you? Because that's the life we live. That is literally our first thought when we wake up. We're just waiting to die. None of us are truly living. We wake. We hunt. We die. That's our life. That's all we have. But we can have more.

Someone just has to step up, to shout from the rooftops that this lifestyle is ridiculous, that the feud is pointless. Someone just needs to believe."

From my pedestal, I see them side-eye each other—cautiously, carefully, and so slowly it's like no one wants to be the first to look the other way, to break my eye contact and meet the gaze of their supposed enemy. But they all do it. Every single one of them. For a brief moment, they look at each other, and I let myself believe my words are finally affecting them. The idea of a good, long life is sinking in.

A sparkle of optimism flashes among them, and it ignites something inside me I was certain I lost long ago: hope. When I look at them now, it's almost as if they all want the same thing: peace. That's all I've ever asked for. But I see their fear too. They're all so scared to actually accept the idea of a different world, of a different lifestyle. They lived this way for so long. I think they fear change more than each other.

"Now, I don't know about any of you, but I have no intention of dying today. I plan to face my father and end his reign of terror once and for all. Darkhaven will not fall to him. And I believe we can do it. I believe we have enough brains, enough experience, enough magic in this room to stop them. But if we can't put our differences aside for this one battle..."

I exhale sharply. That hope I felt only minutes ago is diminishing, and as much as I hate to admit it, fear consumes me.

"Jasik is counting on us," I say, making eye contact with the vampires.

"Darkhaven is counting on us." This time, I look at Aurelia, and I do not break eye contact until she nods.

"It's time you make a decision," I say. "Either you are in,

or you are out. You must be committed to this fight. Being part of this team doesn't mean you act friendly in this room and rebel outside these walls. We need to support each other on the battlefield too.

"Look at the people in this room. Make eye contact with someone different from you. If a rogue vampire is charging that witch or that vampire, are you prepared to step in and save each other? If you answered anything but yes, leave now. You're useless to this cause. That hesitation will get someone killed. Maybe even you."

# SEVEN

$B$ack outside, I take several breaths to quell my budding frustration. I remind myself that anger is useless in war. We don't need egos. We need strategy if we plan to beat an army of rogue vampires that outnumber us by the hundreds. I think about that number again, letting it linger. The longer it sits with me, the more anxious I become.

Hundreds.

There are hundreds of rogue vampires waiting for my father to order our annihilation.

Maybe even more. Maybe there are thousands.

Thousands of rogue vampires giddy with excitement at the thought of killing any living thing it comes into contact with.

They believe Darkhaven doesn't have a chance. Sometimes, I think they're right.

But I can't let the others see that. I need them to trust that we can do this.

Because this misfit group of vampires and witches is Darkhaven's last line of defense.

I sigh heavily, and as much as I try not to think about our impending doom, I can't stop myself. There's nothing quite as humbling as facing one's death. Unfortunately, this experience is something I know well. After all, a day hasn't gone by when

I haven't been fighting for survival. I've been threatened by friend, by foe, by family . . .

I walk to the edge of the porch, letting the tips of my boots hang over the edge of the steps. How many times have I been here? How many times have I looked into the distance, expecting answers, finding none? The darkness used to speak to me. Now it scares me. It makes me feel like I'm not alone.

I sit on the porch steps, letting my legs dangle in front of me. My boots are scuffed, my jeans torn in a way that makes them look fashionable. But they aren't. Every scrape, every tear, every bloodstain has a memory attached to it. It has a face too. Jasik. My sire. My lover. My reason for this life. I'd be dead already if he hadn't saved me. I think about what he must be feeling now, where he must be. My father is probably torturing him. Not for answers. Not for secrets. For fun.

I shake my head, as if the action alone can clear my mind. If only it were that easy. If only my mind was like a chalkboard and the vision of Jasik bloodied and bruised could be eliminated with the swipe of an eraser. But it can't. He's still there. The idea of him on the verge of death is still . . . there.

I distract myself with the sight before me. The forest that surrounds our property is dark despite the early morning hours. The sun is shining overhead, but still muddled by the moon, its rays don't penetrate the thick wood.

It's springtime now, and as the snow melts, making way for seasonal blooms, the trees are beginning to sprout their own foliage. What should be a beautiful time of year is shrouded in gloom. The branches cast shadows that look like monsters, and as the wind billows, they move, reaching closer.

I swallow hard and look away. I can hear the sea from where I sit, and when I close my eyes, I can see it. It amazes me how this one entity can evoke so many different emotions—and all at the same time.

At the shore, waves roll in soft and smooth. The water is calm and comforting here, but farther out, that same water is deadly. The wind whips up waves that crash into boulders with a vengeance, and each time that rock is assaulted, water sprays overhead, pelting every inch of stone. It's soaked and slick. It's dangerous here. The sea is rough where it meets the cliffside, and those murky depths form riptides that threaten to sink all who enter.

Death is everywhere tonight. It's in the caves, in the forest, in the sea. It's in the imaginations of my friends and the hearts of our enemies.

The gargoyle is at my right. The longer I stare into his light-gray stone eyes, the stronger I feel. I don't know how this is possible, but I'm certainly not questioning it.

I smile at him, brushing my fingertips along the curve of his arm. The sensation sends shock waves straight to my bones. I feel it resonate within me, and I shiver because it stings. But I do not remove my hand. Sometimes, I think he is real, that he is slumbering, and my caress is the only affection he experiences in this hardened state.

I lean against him, resting my head against his cool, rigid form. And even though I know my mind must be playing tricks on me, I think he stiffens, as though he is affected by this unusual kindness. As I grow more confident and less fearful of the shape-shifting outside world, I sit upright, but I never break contact. I continue patting his head and silently thanking him for his unyielding strength.

I've been drawn to the gargoyles ever since I arrived at the manor. Even though I know they are simply stone, they make me feel safe, so I let my inner child believe the legend that says gargoyles are the vampires' daylight protectors, because in these desperate times, we need all the protection we can get.

"That was quite the speech," someone says from behind.

I look over my shoulder to find Malik approaching. He sits beside me. Even though we are on the same step, Malik is still much larger than I am, and his bulky frame still towers over me. I have to look up to meet his eyes.

"Was it a bit much?"

I can't help but feel a little self-conscious and a tad hypocritical. I called for confidence, for strength, for trust, and I can barely keep it together out here. My heart leaps at the sight of shadows. I hear waves and think of death. I can barely keep the thought of a dying Jasik out of my mind. I'm drawing strength from a stone gargoyle. I don't know who should be the motivational speaker for this group, but I doubt I'm the best candidate.

"You tell me," he says, glancing over his shoulder.

I follow his gaze to the open front door. Beyond the dimly lit foyer, I see only darkness. I try to listen to what he hears, but I am greeted by silence.

"They stopped arguing," he says. "So you tell me. Was it a bit much?"

I snort at the idea that my long-winded rant actually brought us all together. For months, I've been asking for peace, and I've gotten resistance in return. More than anything, I'm realizing my time as a vampire is turning me into a cynic.

"You didn't think you could rally the troops?" he asks.

"I had my doubts," I admit.

"Getting here hasn't been easy."

"Sometimes, I wonder if this has been worth it."

Malik remains silent as he frowns at me. I'm not sure if he's mentally processing my confession or simply waiting for me to explain myself. Either way, he waits for me to continue, so I try my best to choose my words carefully.

"Sometimes I wonder if trying to bridge the gap between us and them was worth the cost," I say. "We've lost so much, and I can't help but think that things would be different if we just kept to ourselves."

"We can't change the past, Ava. You have a lot of years left. Don't spend them burdening yourself with regret."

I can't help but hear the one thing he is trying hard not to say. He doesn't deny my fear, because he too believes things might be different. Maybe Amicia would be alive. Maybe Jasik would still be here. Maybe the covens wouldn't be dead. Maybe we'd all be . . . happy.

"I didn't understand back then," I say, voice whisper soft. "But I do now."

"You did good work tonight. Focus on that. Focus on how tonight will alter the course of our lives forever."

"That's what I'm worried about."

"I meant that as a positive," Malik says, smiling. "When did you become a pessimist?"

I think about his question, but I'm not sure when pessimism started to overrule optimism. Maybe it was when my grandmother murdered Amicia or when my father killed my mother. Maybe it was when Jasik was abducted while I slept beside him. Or maybe it was when I was so consumed by the black onyx crystal, I tried to kill my friends, an innocent, this entire town. Bad decisions compounded by more bad decisions.

I'm not sure when I became so cynical, but I know it hasn't

been long since doubt started to creep in. I am surrounded by death and doubt. It's all I see, all I feel . . .

"Believe it or not, I'm actually feeling positive about this plan," Malik says.

"It'll never work," I say softly.

He stiffens beside me. I pick at the loose stitching of a tear in my jeans, twisting thread between my thumb and index finger. I feel his gaze on me, but I don't meet his eyes. I'm embarrassed by this confession, even though my shame makes it no less true.

Malik doesn't respond. I imagine he's still reeling from the emotional whiplash I'm putting him through. Only moments ago, I feigned enough confidence to eliminate the division between our groups. I tricked them all. Even him.

"It won't be enough," I say, resorting to honesty. "There are too many of them. Not enough of us."

"With the spell, we have a chance."

"We don't. That's why they keep arguing, because deep down, they all know we're doomed."

"What happened to that girl inside?" Malik asks. "The one who said we needed to trust in this plan, to stay strong for this cause, to believe in each other. Where did she go? What changed since you walked outside?"

Nothing changed, but he won't understand that. I'm still as confused and afraid as I was when I first returned to the manor. I know what we're facing. I saw them. I stared into the abyss, and a thousand red eyes stared back at me. As much as I want to win, I don't think we can. Not like this. We're missing something. We need . . . more. More power. More allies. More magic.

"I said what needed to be said to keep them on track."

"But you still don't believe? You're still convinced this plan will fail?"

"There are hundreds of them, Malik. Maybe more. There are four of us. It's simple math."

"You think the witches won't join us?"

"I think they will, but they'll need time to perform the ritual. They'll be vulnerable during that time, and they'll rely on us to keep them safe."

"We can do that," Malik says. "We've kept Darkhaven safe for centuries."

"Against a few rogues, sure. But against an army? Against hundreds? We can't. Four isn't enough."

He doesn't respond. He doesn't need to. His silence screams. I can sense his frustration, his fury, his annoyance. With the others finally on track, the last thing he needs is to get me back on board. But keeping my thoughts to myself isn't an option. Malik needs to know how dangerous this will be.

"I'll still fight," I say.

"But fighting without hope . . ." He sighs heavily, shaking his head.

He sounds almost . . . defeated. I did this to him. I took his optimism and infected him with my own fear. I might be right. Without more vampires, we're doomed, but maybe I approached this issue all wrong.

I grab his hand, locking my fingers with his.

He squeezes me gently and offers a weak smile that doesn't reach his eyes.

"I have hope," I lie.

"Do you?"

"Trust me, I want nothing more than for this to end in our favor. I just think we need to be smart about this. That's all. We need a better plan."

"A better plan than using the most powerful magic we have against vampires?"

I know he's referencing the sun, and he's right. It is the witches' best chance at facing an army of rogue vampires. Without it, they wouldn't last long in this fight. Rogues are naturally stronger, faster. They best even us at times. The witches don't stand a chance without the sun spell.

"The sun spell is for them," I say. "We need a better plan for us."

I need him to know I am on his side, that he can count on me. I would follow him to the end of the world—even if that's tonight. Malik might not feel like much of a leader, but to me, he is. Taking over for Amicia couldn't have been easy, and now that his brother is missing, the last thing he needs is my brutal honesty. So I'll put on a brave face and figure out how the hell we're going to survive this on my own. In silence.

"Should I take patrol?" I ask, hoping a change in subject will break his stoicism.

"Jeremiah should be patrolling right now."

There is uncertainty in his voice, and I know why. He's right. Jeremiah is supposed to be patrolling, but he's not. I can smell him. He's nearby. Maybe on the side of the house where the wraparound porch ends at a bench.

Malik and I are both silent now as we focus on him.

Holland is there. They speak in whispers.

I shuffle to my feet and begin walking to the edge of the porch, but just before I round the corner, where they are certain to see me, I am stopped.

Malik's hand is wrapped around my arm. He shakes his head sternly and tries to usher me back inside. There is a long-standing agreement in this house that we don't use our heightened senses to invade privacy unless absolutely necessary. I suppose curiosity as to why he isn't patrolling when he should be doesn't qualify as an urgent matter.

I don't take more than a few steps backward before I comprehend what they are saying. Jeremiah's plea rushes through me, piercing my heart. I gasp, unable to believe what I am hearing.

"We can use the eclipse," Jeremiah says.

"I can't believe what you're suggesting," Holland hisses. "These are our friends!"

"It isn't safe here," Jeremiah says. "Not anymore."

"We have a plan, Jer. We have the witches. I can make this spell work."

"I know you can," Jeremiah says, voice calm and soft. "But we're out of blood, and there is an army of rogue vampires on their way. We're talking about suicide."

I can't help but make comparisons. Jeremiah and I have come to the same conclusions. Facing the rogue army with our current plan is suicide, but our decisions after that realization couldn't be more different. I'd never just abandon my friends.

"They need us," Holland says.

"This isn't our fight," Jeremiah answers.

"Jasik needs you. He's like a brother to you!"

"He needs a miracle. And I'm fresh out."

I clench my jaw, grinding my teeth as I listen to their argument. My breath is loud and shaky, and I'm surprised they can't hear it.

What really makes my blood boil is that I trusted him. Despite our differences and recently shaky friendship, I trusted Jeremiah, and I can count on one hand the number of people I would trust with my life. I guess it's one less now.

"I just—I can't..." Holland struggles to find the right words, and I don't blame him. I'm struggling to understand as well. "I can't believe what I'm hearing."

"You're all I care about," Jeremiah says. "I can't worry about them too."

With his last confession, I rip my arm free from Malik and stomp my feet until I'm around the corner. I want them to hear me coming, to be absolutely sure I overheard everything they said. We don't have time for liars.

I make eye contact with Jeremiah, silently daring him to tell me to my face that the vampire he has spent his entire immortal life with is better off without him.

Jeremiah's eyes widen at the sight of me, and I close the space between us. We're less than a foot away from each other now, inhaling each other's air with every angry breath.

"This is about me, isn't it?" I ask.

I don't bother to confirm what we both know. Yes, I heard what he said, and no, Malik can't stop me from confronting him. If he wants to leave Jasik for dead, then he'll need to tell me that to my face. Sneaking out under the security of dusk is coward's play. If he plans to be a deserter, he'll say it outright.

Like Jeremiah, I might have doubts about our plan. I too might believe we're all going to die if we don't do something about it, but I would never just walk away. I would never leave the others to fend for themselves. This is about family, about duty and honor. These must be foreign concepts to Jeremiah.

"What are you talking about?" Jeremiah asks. "This has nothing to do with you."

He is stern with me. His usual happy, laid-back personality is replaced by his malice. He doesn't speak to me the way he speaks to Holland, and that's okay. I'm starting to hate him just a little bit too. And that's a lot easier to do when he's not faking nice.

"This is because of what I did," I say. "When I hurt you."

Succumbing to the entity within the black onyx crystal wasn't my proudest moment. If I hadn't been stopped, I would have killed them all. I will regret my actions for the rest of my life, even if I had no real control over them, but Jeremiah can't take his anger with me out on Jasik. It's not right. It's not fair.

"This has nothing to do with you, Ava," Jeremiah says. "This is about us. Holland and I have a chance if we leave now."

"I can't believe you'd just walk away. After everything—"

"Ava," Malik says.

His tone silences me. It is immediate and all-consuming. With a numb tongue, I cease my fight with Jeremiah and turn to face my leader. Already, I know I will abide by his wishes.

Malik is standing only a few feet behind me. His body is rigid, his form towering. His jaw is squared, his arms two muscular limbs crossed over his chest. Completely emotionless, he is closing himself off to us. Again. After all, this is his signature look, the one that used to scare me because it was so unreadable, like a robot, like he wasn't even real.

But the more time I spent with him, the better I became at seeing past the facade. I became an expert at seeing his true colors, at reading the emotions he didn't want the others to know were there. Except for now. Because now, there is a wall around him. I can almost see it being erected, brick by brick, and somehow, I just know I won't break through. Not this time.

"Malik . . ." I whisper.

I reach for him, fingertips just barely grazing his skin, before he turns on his heels and walks toward the front door. He disappears around the corner, and even though I know he isn't gone forever, that I can go inside and he'll still be there, something has changed. The dynamic of our nest has shifted, and I fear we'll never be the same again.

# EIGHT

The tension inside is unbearable. Jeremiah's betrayal cut deep, but somehow, the quiet is even worse. It screams at me, clawing my insides, shredding flesh, leaving me as nothing more than a pile of scraps. It makes me want to scream. But I don't. I suffer in silence.

The others overheard Jeremiah's admission, and I wonder where their loyalty will fall. The witches are already uneasy, wondering if they're making the right choice. I don't blame them. Just yesterday, we were enemies. If the vampires begin their retreat, the witches are sure to follow.

Perhaps Hikari will want to go with them, leaving only Malik and me to free Jasik. Perhaps the three of us will die together. If it's my time, that's how I'd want it to happen. I'd want to go down fighting for what's right. I might not foil my father's plan, but I'll take some of his allies with me.

A knock at the door startles us. We're all caught off guard, which isn't an easy feat. The combination of the four of us equals pretty spectacularly heightened senses, so I can't help the immediate dread that washes over me.

How did someone get so close without us knowing?

I think of the witches. I don't want to place blame, especially without proof, but the thoughts that consume me are of fake allegiances and a Trojan horse.

Are they really here to help us? Or are they just more witches converted by my father? We already know he's capable of that. He convinced Sofía to murder her entire family to prove her loyalty to my father. Who knows what he made these witches promise him?

I shake my head, as if the gesture alone can clear my mind. It doesn't work, so I remind myself that only a few hours ago, I stood here and chastised those unwilling to work together. I put on a brave face in that moment. I tried to channel great leaders, offer moving words of wisdom. It might have worked on them, but inside, I still have my doubts. And now, I can't shake the feeling that my insecurities will come back to bite me later.

I look for Malik, and I find him seething near the fireplace in the parlor. He doesn't notice me, though. His attention is solely on Jeremiah. This behavior is becoming quite the norm for Malik. He does not bother to hide his anger. My leader is furious, and I understand why. Jeremiah was supposed to be on patrol. Instead, he was planning a coup. Had he not intended to abandon us all, he would have been scouring the woods. He would have sensed an intruder and warned us before they got this close.

There is another knock at the front door—louder now. It echoes through the manor as we all stare dumbfounded at each other. I know we need to act quickly, to form a defense, but like the others, I don't move. I can't. I'm frozen in time, feet glued to the hardwood floor. This really isn't a shining moment for us.

We know we're not ready. We can't survive a fight. Not yet. Not without a spell, without the orbs, without an actual plan to save our lives. My throat swells, and it's hard to breathe. My pulse is racing. If the others hear it, they do not acknowledge the sheer panic rising in my chest.

Malik and Jeremiah are arguing, but my ears are ringing. I can barely hear them. Their words come in choppy bits.

"... watching the door!" Malik shouts.

"... more important things ..." Jeremiah responds.

I think Malik tells him that we need him, that we are relying on his help, that the witches came to us for protection and to aid in our battle. But the look on Jeremiah's face tells me he doesn't care. Not anymore.

It's Jeremiah's revelation that finally grounds me.

"Admit it, Malik," Jeremiah hisses. "We're screwed. Amicia is dead. We all know she was the strongest. Now Jasik is missing, and our enemy has an amulet powerful enough to cause an eclipse."

Malik attempts to intervene, but Jeremiah doesn't stop. Instead, he silences our leader with the wave of his hand.

"We are starving and exhausted," Jeremiah says. "No one actually cares about patrolling the woods right now because it doesn't matter. When the rogues decide it's time to show up, they will. And we all know we can't stop them. If they want inside this house, they'll get in."

"He's right," a witch says, stepping forward. "We're all going to die. Everyone knows that."

The girl speaking looks no older than a teenager, and I can't help but wonder how she got caught up in this mess, how any of us got here.

The signs were there. I see them now when I look back at the months I've lived as a vampire. My father was there. Always. Testing me. Seeing my capabilities. Biding time until it was advantageous for him to attack.

How did we not see it? How did I not know he was alive? How did I not sense his presence?

They say you can sense a loved one. You can feel when something goes wrong. I've read those unbelievable stories about a mother in New York and a daughter in California. Somehow, the mother can feel the exact moment of her daughter's car accident, despite being several thousand miles away. It's supposedly possible. A sixth sense. If anyone were to have this bonus ability, it should be me.

If my father was here, in Darkhaven, how did I not feel him? With heightened senses and vampire strength and witch magic and immortality, I still couldn't feel what mere mortals could.

There is another knock at the door, and this time, I hear the aggression. Whoever wants in is getting annoyed by our silence. They know we're in here, and it's only a matter of time before they enter uninvited.

Malik storms off in frustration. He moves so quickly, so swiftly, he appears to be gliding, like he's hovering over the floor, fueled solely by his anger and the wind. He reaches the foyer just as I find my legs and chase after him.

I call out, but he ignores me.

Jeremiah may be right. A wood door is no match for a rogue army. If they want inside, they'll get in here. We can't really stop them. Not for long, anyway. But that doesn't mean we need to be reckless. There are enough witches here to throw up a boundary spell to distract the rogues long enough to make our escape. It's not much, but it's better than nothing. And nothing is all he has right now.

Malik opens the door with such ferocity, it slams into the wall and shatters the stained-glass insert.

Our visitor gasps, nearly dropping the bright-red cooler in her hands. She takes several steps backward, stopping as the heel of her foot hangs over the top step. Any farther, and she would have tumbled down the stairs and to the ground. The last thing we need right now is to take care of an injured human.

What is she even doing here? And how did she find us? She's seen us emerge and disappear into the forest, but Darkhaven's woods are vast. There's no way she could just happen upon the manor. Not without decent knowledge of tracking.

"Luna?" My shock leaves my word nothing more than a whisper, but it's enough for Malik to overhear.

The shopkeeper doesn't respond. In fact, her gaze never leaves Malik. She clutches the hard cooler against her chest, using it as a barrier between her and the house full of vampires—as if that alone could stop him, or the others, from reaching her.

Maybe she'll just throw it at him, like the time she threw a jar of garlic at me. Honestly, that might work. He'll be stunned, that's for sure.

Malik visibly softens at the sight of her. He reaches an arm out, and she hisses.

I suppress a chuckle, because despite the amusing scene playing out before me, our situation is fairly dire. There's nothing funny about impending doom—not even when it's interrupted by a mortal hissing like a cat at a vampire who is at least four times larger than her.

"I'm sorry," Malik says. "I didn't mean to startle you."

Despite my snort, he seems unfazed by her reaction. He has been around a lot longer than me. Maybe hissing is a typical reaction from humans who are aware that vampires exist. It reminds me of how cats used to be the guardians in Egypt because the dead were afraid of them. A cat stopped a reincarnated mummy in that one movie. Maybe it holds power over us too. After all, we're just as dead.

Malik strides toward her. Her voice lowers, deepens, and when he's within an arm's reach of her, I am absolutely certain that hiss has turned into a growl. This stops him dead in his tracks. He tosses a glance over his shoulder at me, and I shrug.

I think it's safe to say this is the first time a human being has growled at Malik. Apparently, hissing he can handle, but not growling.

Luna's only response is to thrust the cooler at Malik. Stunned, he fumbles as he grabs onto it and stumbles backward a bit. I find a moment of amusement when I think about my earlier theory—that Luna planned to use that cooler as a weapon against the leader of this nest.

If she retreats now, while he's distracted by figuring out what the heck is going on, she might actually get away. Not that she needs to. The only danger here is in her mind. Malik would never hurt her, but I guess she doesn't know that.

Malik looks from the cooler to Luna several times, as if his blatant confusion is enough for her to explain herself.

She doesn't.

"What's in the cooler, Luna?" I ask.

I am standing directly beside Malik now. She still hasn't looked at me, but she responds.

"I thought you might be hungry," she says softly.

Her voice is weak and strained, husky and dry. I've never seen her like this before. Even when I tried to kill her, she kept it together better than this. I can't tell if she's afraid or aroused. It amuses me.

I glance between the two and feel a strange spark forming. Despite the fact that Luna did answer me and they're both aware that I am standing right here, it feels like I'm witnessing something I shouldn't see, like I'm intruding on their personal time and space. There's something intimate about the way they stare into each other's eyes, both unwilling or unable to break the spell.

"You brought us blood?" I ask, frowning.

Somehow, I am certain this is the first time in vampire history that a human willingly shows up at a vampire's house with blood offerings. This seems like one of those dangerous situations they typically avoid in the movies.

She nods. "I thought you might be hungry," she says, repeating herself.

Her eyes are still glued to Malik, and their staring contest is starting to become uncomfortable. I contemplate walking away and leaving them alone for the sole purpose of seeing if anyone notices. At this point, I don't think they would.

Malik has seen Luna before, but in those times, emotions were high. We were either fighting for our lives or with each other, so I understand why her unnatural allure hasn't affected him until this moment, when she's all he can see. But even though I sympathize with him and have been there myself, we're pressed for time. We can't spend what little remains obsessing over the new chick.

Hopefully, when this is over, we'll all still be around, and we can sit down and chat about that one time they had an awkward, likely record-breaking staring contest.

Since they have yet to respond, or blink, I make the first move. I open the cooler and find around a dozen clear plastic containers. On each lid, a few different dates have been written in small, bold-font letters. The scratchy writing is hard to read, but I can make out that the contents in all containers seem to be from this week.

"Where did you get the blood?" I ask.

She doesn't respond. I glance between the two, frustration rising. Again, I remind myself that I understand why he is mesmerized. I was too. It takes some time to get used to her scent. There is something about her that just draws me in. Now that I see Malik's reaction to her, when he can focus on her and nothing else, I'm happy to know she doesn't only affect me this way. But that makes being around us all the more dangerous for her.

"Luna?" I ask. "Where did you get this?"

"The butcher," she says.

Luna speaks slowly, mindlessly, like a drone.

Unable to stand this any longer, I snap my fingers at her several times. I'm overwhelmed by shame, but they're giving me the creeps. I reacted strangely too, but I still had my bearings. I wasn't a drooling, dry-eyed fool.

Despite feeling bad for snapping at her, it worked. She tears her gaze away from Malik in a way that looks physically painful. It's like she's fighting to free herself from this spell.

"You guys are starting to freak me out," I say.

This makes her blink several times. Her eyes are still blank, but at least they're focused on me. She frowns and arches a brow at my confession. She doesn't understand what I'm talking about. I don't think she's fully aware that they have been awkwardly staring at each other for several minutes now, and I can't help but want to roll my eyes at the universe for sending yet another problem I'll have to fix. I really, really don't have time for this.

"So the butcher just gave this to you?" I ask, hoping for a subject change.

"He throws away whole tubs of that stuff every day," she says with a nod. "You really should take advantage of that. He sells it for cheap."

"He didn't think it was weird that you requested a dozen containers of animal blood?"

"Everyone in Darkhaven thinks I'm weird. I think he assumed it was for the shop."

"Well..."

I suppose she's right. Despite the fact that Darkhaven was founded by the supernatural, not everyone in town is magical. The butcher is human, and when the store owner of an occult shop asks to buy blood, I guess his natural reaction would be to assume it's for Lunar Magic.

"Thank you," I say. "Your timing is impeccable."

She smiles at me, beaming widely. I can almost see the nerdy, shy yet confident girl I used to know behind those eyes. Maybe I'm the one seeing things. Maybe her interaction with Malik wasn't all that weird after all.

My hand is still resting on the cooler, and as Malik wavers unsteadily on his feet, the dark crimson liquid swishes inside each cup.

I lick my lips in response. Just by looking at it, I can already taste the thick liquid, can already smell the sweet aroma. My stomach growls, and even though I have recently eaten, I am absolutely certain I could drink each one of these on my own.

I close the lid, pushing it down so hard, Malik teeters forward.

He steadies himself by stepping even closer to Luna.

She gasps, and I can tell Malik is acutely aware of that short, quick inhalation.

His eyes are on her lips, her throat, and the sound of her overworked heart hammers between them.

She swallows hard, and the sound of her muscles contracting makes a soft squishing sound. The moonlight is bathing her silhouette in a bright light. It bounces off her pale skin, her stark black hair, her bright eyes. She isn't wearing her glasses tonight. This is the first time I've seen her without them.

Luna really is strikingly beautiful. It isn't just her scent that pulls me in. Her features do as well.

Finally, finally, Malik speaks, though I am not yet convinced he's completely back to normal.

"How did you find us?" Malik asks, voice slow and steady, unlike his footing and shaking arms.

"It wasn't really that hard," she responds. "Ava offered little clues during our time together."

"Clues?" I ask, thinking back.

I can't remember ever telling her where the manor was located. She might have seen me retreat into the woods, but the forest is vast. It would take a skilled tracker or someone with heightened senses to find us without actual directions. I mean, there are still rogue vampires who can't find our nest. So how did she?

"I guess you were getting worse at keeping your guard up around me," she says.

I narrow my eyes at this. For the first time since we met, Luna is giving me bad vibes. The red flags are glaring—from her weird connection with Malik, to her showing up uninvited with blood, to her always having the answers we need right when we need them. What do we really know about her? I befriended her out of necessity, and now I'm wondering who I let into my life.

"Should I have kept my guard up?" I ask.

Luna scrunches her nose as she shakes her head, and it makes her look like a child. Her hair moves with her, flowing back and forth, until it cascades over her shoulders. She smiles widely at me, teeth eerily white and shiny in this half-night darkness, and I can't help thinking about the wolf that pretended to be the grandmother in that children's story.

With Luna's gaze focused on me, Malik seems to have broken free. He clears his throat and blinks several times. He steps backward, leaving me alone as he slowly retreats toward the manor. He stops when he's standing in the doorway, safely tucked on the other side of the threshold.

"Of course not, Ava," Luna says. "We're friends."

I don't miss the strange, sweet-sounding, singsong tone to her voice—almost like the wolf when it spoke to the granddaughter just before it ate her.

# NINE

Back inside, I keep a watchful eye on Luna. Something has changed since we were outside. In the span of just a few minutes, her demeanor has completely shifted. Once again, she's that kind, quirky shopkeeper I remember her to be. It's as if that weird hex I witnessed outside lifted the moment she stepped inside the manor. She's smiling and friendly. I respond defiantly, by narrowing my eyes at her. It's petty, but it makes me feel in control. And I need a win right now.

The wolf—for the moment, anyway—seems to have retreated.

Still, I can't shake the feeling that something is amiss, like Luna is hiding a secret far darker than anything we're prepared to face.

Over the years, I've learned to trust my instincts, as they rarely betray me, but I wonder if I'm worrying for nothing. Am I overthinking this? Has my father poisoned my trust in others? I'd like to think I'm just paranoid because the last person to infiltrate our nest turned out to be a spy working for him.

I remind myself that Sofía gave me weird vibes too, and the others ignored them. She was welcomed into our home, and now, Jasik is missing, and my father has the amulet. Luna could be just as diabolical. I should assume the worst. But as I look at her now, watching as she visibly shrinks under the gaze of the magical community, I actually sympathize with her.

My emotions for this girl are erratic, making stressing over Luna utterly exhausting, and what's worse is I can't share my feelings with anyone.

I sigh heavily, catching Holland's attention.

He arches a brow in curiosity and frowns at me. He speaks with his eyes, asking me what is wrong, but I don't respond. I just smile. If it were a normal day with normal problems, I might seek advice, but for now, I need his focus on the spell. Saving Jasik and stopping my father must be our priority. As much as I hate putting off an interrogation, Luna's agenda will have to wait for another day.

Seemingly unaware of my internal turmoil, Malik approaches me, arm extended, fingers wrapped around the base of a plastic container. In one hand, he carries the cooler. In the other, a blood offering. The crimson liquid sloshes from side to side, staining the plastic a light-pink hue. My stomach growls at the sight, but I know I am not hungry. Of everyone here, I ate most recently.

I shake my head, stopping him short as I wave him off with my hand.

"You need to eat," he says.

"I did eat," I remind him. "Give that to the others."

I ready myself for protest, but he surprises me by turning on his heels and walking away. Perhaps he too is over the dramatics of this day. I don't blame him. We've been arguing for hours. I'm over it too.

Malik divvies the blood supply among the other vampires, handing each hunter two containers. They don't ask questions, and they don't wait to drink. In loud, greedy slurps, the cartons are emptied. Bellies are full, and once again, our fridge is empty.

Jeremiah licks his lips, eyes focused on the empty plastic cups in his hands. He places one inside the other and closes his fist around them, crushing both. The sound is loud and sharp, and it quickly fills the room.

No one speaks, but everyone watches.

"This won't be enough," he mutters.

He speaks slowly, calmly, and even though his voice is low in volume, I know it's all anyone can hear. He speaks the truth, but brutal honesty is the last thing we need right now. We need hope and faith. But our hope for a better future is fizzling out, and we lost our faith a long time ago. His honesty only makes everything worse.

"It's better than nothing," I say, hoping he'll take the hint.

He doesn't.

"We'll still starve without more."

"Perhaps you should focus on appreciating what you do have," Malik says.

"This is enough to keep emotions in check," Hikari adds. "To keep the insanity at bay."

She hasn't spoken much since we agreed to save Jasik and battle my father. It's unlike her not to voice her opinions, and I feared that she would side with Jeremiah and leave us to fight alone. But maybe I was wrong about her. Maybe I'm wrong about everyone . . .

I glance at Luna. She stands alone, watching as the vampires argue about the blood she just provided them. My annoyance grows at how ungrateful we must seem. They haven't even thanked her. She risked her life to get that blood, to bring it here, not knowing how we would react or what evils might be lurking in these woods. We're hardly the only vampires around.

She opens her mouth to speak, but no sound escapes. She closes her mouth and tries again. She does this several times. I wait for her confidence to grow, not wanting to push her into whatever speech she seems to have planned. Malik and I both failed miserably when we tried to sway Jeremiah to our side. Perhaps this outsider knows the words needed to convince everyone that we have a chance, that there is hope. Maybe her faith is enough.

Or maybe she's about to tell us what I feared. That she has some deep, dark secret, and we're all doomed.

I roll my eyes and groan internally. My emotions are giving me whiplash. I run a hand through my hair, only now noticing it's a tangled mess. I try to remember the last time I showered and come up blank. Like my trust, my memory is failing me too.

"We'll be fine with this," Hikari says.

"For now . . . maybe," Jeremiah says.

"Jer . . ." Holland says, voice low and strained.

His jaw is clenched tightly as he shakes his head at Jeremiah. His eyes are hard, dark pebbles that stare angrily at his lover. I appreciate the fact that I am not the only one with a growing sense of annoyance. Jeremiah might want to leave, but it seems Holland does not. Maybe he will be convinced to stay after all. He might be okay with abandoning us, but I doubt he'll leave Holland.

A shuffling to my right catches my attention, and I realize the witches have been staring at Luna since she arrived. Their sideways glances are painfully obvious, as is the disdain in their eyes, but I've been more focused on her intentions than their curiosity. I'm sure they find it strange for a human to visit a vampire nest.

There has always been an unspoken agreement among vampires and witches. We keep the secret. Humans can never know. They assumed we kept our end of the deal, but the truth is out. Luna knows.

So far, they haven't voiced their concern, but I can tell this moment of silence won't last long. They are reaching their boiling point and soon will burst. It's inevitable.

The truth that a human knows about us will create quite the frenzy among the witches, and it'll derail our entire plan to save Darkhaven. I can't allow that, so I need to distract everyone from Luna's presence... but how?

Unfortunately, Aurelia beats me to the punch.

"You have *humans* bringing you blood?" she hisses.

I can tell by her tone that she was itching to ask this question. She kept quiet while the vampires continued their petty argument about the amount of blood gifted and watched as Luna struggled to speak to us.

In the eyes of mortals, this looks bad. Not only do we have a human courier who is clearly too scared to speak in front of us, but we have also committed the ultimate sin against the supernatural community when we invited Luna into our home and showed her our truth.

In their eyes, this is unforgivable.

Aurelia's hair is as fiery red and feral as her anger. It shakes wildly as she makes eye contact with every... single... vampire... in the room. It's a bit dramatic for my taste, but I understand her emphasis. She's waiting for a response, for an explanation, because she believes this delivery system is common.

It's not, but she'll never believe this is Luna's first time here. And if it were, we'd lie, and then she'd have no reason to believe us when we tell the truth.

Once again, I sigh and think long and hard about how I'm going to fix yet another mess. It's all I can seem to do lately. Sigh and breathe. Grunt and groan. Put out fires and try not to start more.

I close my eyes and pinch the bridge of my nose, focusing on that tiny little voice in my mind that's telling me I am on the verge of an emotional breakdown. I can't let my anger get the best of me. Rage never helps a situation, and it certainly won't convince the witches to stay. And as much as I hate to admit it, we need them. Whatever ritual Holland concocts will rely on their magical strength as a full coven. I can't let them leave.

When I open my eyes again, I find Luna staring at me. Her gaze is sympathetic, her smile sweet and sincere. It makes my heart soften. This is the girl I remember. The new friend I made who helped me through some of my recent tough times. Without her help, and her trust, we wouldn't have gotten this far. Her tomes and the Orb of Helios will save us all. I'm sure of that.

She tears her vision from mine and blinks several times. I can hear her erratic heartbeat, her heavy breathing. Each inhalation sounds like a freight train in my mind. It is loud and constant, and the slow, steady chug of air makes it impossible to hear the others. Her body goes stiff as she stands tall, sticking out her chest and angling her jaw forward at an awkward angle.

When she shouts, the room silences, and for several seconds, all I hear is the strained beats of her exhausted heart.

"Just. Stop. Fighting!" Luna yells, emphasizing each word.

Shame washes over the group at once. The same look is painted across their faces, but they all handle it differently.

Jeremiah crosses his arms over his chest in defiance.

DARK REIN

Hikari kicks at the floor with a scuffed boot. Malik stares into the distance, avoiding all eye contact. Aurelia clears her throat. Another rolls her eyes.

"Darkhaven is under attack," Luna says. "Before I got blood from the butcher, I visited the hospital. It's on the verge of collapse. They are overwhelmed by mysterious cases. Animal attacks. That's what they're calling them. Dozens come in by the hour. At this rate, there won't be anyone left. Darkhaven will be a ghost town."

As I listen, I gnaw on my lower lip, growing increasingly nervous with each word she speaks. By their worried glances, I can tell the others are just as concerned as I am, because we all know what this means.

Since humans aren't privy to our existence, rogue vampire bites are often mislabeled as animal attacks. Rogues are ruthless in their hunt. When they feed, they don't simply bite down and wait for blood to flow, leaving only two tiny puncture holes. They savagely tear through flesh, ripping straight to the bone. It does look like an animal attack, and the sad truth is, the rogues' lack of self-control has protected us. They kill without mercy. If they fed as we do, clean and precise, humans would have been on to us long ago. There would be no denying the existence of vampires.

The increase in attacks, the murder of innocents, the intention to form a ghost town, can only mean one thing: my father is making his move.

And we're not ready.

# TEN

I was young when I was informed of my birthright, and as a child, I didn't fully understand it then. Mamá simply told me that I was different. When I told her I could *feel* the earth, *hear* its cries, she believed me. She told me that one day, I would be able to answer it, and in that moment, I would summon... *magic*.

I didn't really know what magic was. The concept was far too complex for my tiny mind. But I saw the way her eyes glistened at the word. I saw how she smiled brightly when she talked to me about it. And that only made me want magic more. Unfortunately, I didn't romanticize magic for long.

I was a teenager when I learned that magic came with responsibility—a responsibility few are forced to bear. The truth came during a failed mission. I was supposed to track a vampire that made Darkhaven its hunting grounds, but as an unexperienced witch, I was too late to stop it.

The vampire escaped before I even found it that night, so I never saw its face. When I think about this now, I wonder if it was *him*. My father. Hunting. Killing. Maiming in the very place I loved. It was on this night, when I encountered the bloodbath he left behind, that the truth revealed itself to me.

My birthright wasn't just magic. It was responsibility. Because those who have power must protect those who do not.

This is a lesson *all* witches learn, so I find it disheartening that they are eager to retreat now. Explaining the irony will likely anger them more, making their abandonment a certainty, so I don't speak on that. Instead, I decide to answer their ridiculous questions as simply as I can.

"This isn't what we signed up for," a witch says.

I don't bother making eye contact, so I'm not sure who spoke. I recognize the voice as yet another naysayer, another doubter. Like the others, she is cynical and rash in her assumptions.

"On the contrary," I say, "fighting rogue vampires is *exactly* what you signed up for."

"We've been here for *hours*," she adds, "and nothing has happened. We're still just as lost and unsure as we were when we arrived."

I look at her now. She is middle-aged. Petite. Even shorter than me, and I don't consider myself very tall. Her frame looks sickly thin, and I wonder if she's even strong enough to fight. Her hair is beginning to gray, giving her a salt-and-pepper look. Her eyes are sunken, her skin wrinkled. She reminds me of my mother.

"I don't agree," I say. "We have the orbs. We are working on a spell. We have a plan."

The constant arguing and dismissive attitudes are clouding her judgment. With a proper ritual and a spell or two, we have more than enough power to face his army. But she can't see that. All she sees are petty vampires complaining over the blood supply, one of our own contemplating leaving, a human in our midst, and the lingering doubt hanging over the group. She's giving up, and I can't seem to shout the words to beg her not to.

"We are wasting time siding with the enemy," she says.

She is seething now. Her anger over what's happening to Darkhaven is misplaced. She should take out this frustration on my father, on his rogue army, not on us. And the best way to do that is to end this fight with a bang—like some epic action sequence in a blockbuster movie. At least, that's how I see it. That's how I want to go out.

With. A. Bang.

"We aren't your enemy," I remind her.

Even though I try not to, I think I upset her even more. Her cheeks redden, eyes narrow. She inhales through her nose, and the sound is loud and constant, almost like she never even exhales. She blinks several times as the silence stretches between us, both waiting for the other to break first.

"We should be protecting our own," she says.

"We want to protect them too."

At this, she snorts. She turns away, and now I'm certain she hates me. She faces Aurelia, and even though no words are spoken between them, I know something is being said. They speak with their eyes, but the conversation ends quickly.

"I will not force anyone to stay," Aurelia says. "Make your decision now. Go back to town and fight on your own. Or stay with the vampires and work together. The decision is yours."

I'll admit, I am surprised by her words. I assumed she would leave with the others. Protecting Darkhaven is innate. The desire is rooted so deeply within me, I can't tell where it ends and I begin. I don't even know if my need to save them is because I *want* to or if it's because I was taught to. Either way, it doesn't matter. They need us, and sometimes, that's enough.

The witch turns and leaves, and many follow her. I'm not sure if this is the outcome Aurelia expected, but it's what I foresaw. They believe we are leaving the humans of Darkhaven to fend for themselves, but in reality, the responsibility we feel to defend this town against a destructive and ruthless outsider is just as strong as theirs. They paint us to be the evil ones, but in truth, we've done nothing but fend off their constant attacks. Despite their distaste in our proximity to Darkhaven, this is our home too, and we will not lose it to a tyrant.

One by one, witches storm out of the manor. Only the echoing sound of their retreating footsteps is evidence they were ever here. Silence blankets the room, much like the rush of greenery emerging outside as we are welcomed into a new season. Unfortunately, spring feels a lot like winter. It's dark and dreary, a stark reminder that the world is a painful place and we are left to navigate it alone.

The subtle mist in the air is thick in my lungs, and despite my best efforts to clear the fog, I am never free of it. Just like I am never free of *them*.

No one speaks. We simply stare at the foyer. Much like my bitter heart, it's empty. The bones of this house are hollow, the floors barren, the rooms lifeless eye sockets.

It didn't always look so . . . dead. It wasn't so long ago that Amicia welcomed me here, offered me a home when I was exiled by my own people. This was a lively, happy vampire nest. And then I showed up with decrepit family ties and a string of bad decisions.

The others stare at the foyer with deep strain in their eyes, as if their disbelief can will them back, but their hushed pleas fall on deaf ears. Because the witches are already gone.

I don't bother begging. I simply shake my head. The effort is moot; if they cared about my disapproval, they wouldn't have left to begin with. But it makes me feel better.

I decided to let them go before they even left the room. Because I'm tired. I'm tired of proving ourselves worthy. I'm tired of defending our right to exist. I'm tired of arguing that to win a war, we must stick together. If our actions so far haven't proved this, nothing will.

I turn toward the others and face the few witches who remain. I make eye contact with Jeremiah and frown. I expected him to follow the others, but he didn't. He is standing beside Holland, arms crossed over his chest. His lips are pursed, eyes narrowed. Even though he is angry with us, with this situation, he is choosing to fight with us. Or maybe he refuses to abandon his boyfriend. Either is a win, really. Like the rest, he's another soldier on the front lines.

"We can't just let them leave!"

Luna speaks before I do, and when she does, her sense of urgency is clear.

I feel the panic that rises in her chest as though it were my own. She doesn't understand why we aren't stopping them, why we aren't begging them to stay and fight. And I don't expect her to. She didn't witness the back-and-forth, the cat-and-mouse game we played with them earlier.

How many times did they threaten to leave? How many times did we beg them to stay? Thinking we could work together, that we would be *stronger* together, was childish. Yesterday, we were enemies, and today, we're to be allies? Only a fool would believe someone's heart could change so drastically, so suddenly. The truth is, they made up their minds before they even knocked on our door, and their decision was not in our favor. It never will be.

"We've tried countless times to convince them," I say. "At this point, asking them to stay is just wasting time."

Luna's gaze turns to Malik, and a rush of energy flows between them. He tenses under the full assault of the mysterious magic that links them together. With his jaw clenched shut, he says nothing, but his eyes convey his pain. It's obvious he's just as desperate as she is for the witches' help.

Shaking her head, Luna tears her vision from Malik, and she storms out of the room. As she spins on her heels, her hair whips wildly at her shoulders, each strand lost in its own frenzied whirlwind.

I decide to chase after her before she has even exited the manor, but she's outside before I'm able to reach her and grab hold.

"Leave me alone!" Luna shouts, pulling her arm from my grip.

"It's not safe for you to be in these woods alone," I argue.

"What about the witches who left? Aren't they in danger? Or do you not care about them at all?"

"They can take care of themselves. You can't. You're mortal."

She opens her mouth to speak but clamps it shut before words can escape. Her eyes are narrowed, nostrils flaring as she breathes heavily.

I'm used to her happy-go-lucky demeanor, so her drastic change in attitude has me stumbling backward. Increasing the space between us seems like the safest option right now.

"I don't need your protection," she hisses. "I've lived in Darkhaven all my life, Ava. I can take care of myself."

"Things are different now. You know that. Don't let your pride—"

"Stop treating me like a child!" Luna shouts. "I'm not some weak, absent-minded mortal. I'm—I'm . . ."

She breaks eye contact to kick at the ground. A spray of dirt and pebbles flings forward, scattering across my scuffed boots.

"I imagine it's pretty difficult to be you," I say.

She frowns, and her eyes trail the length of my frame. She's sizing me up, scanning for even the smallest hint of dishonesty.

"I think it'd be hard to be the normal one surrounded by superheroes," I say, snorting at the concept of a superhero even as the word leaves my mouth. "We treat you like a human being because you are one, but in our world, mortality isn't exactly a compliment. It means weakness, and sometimes, the way we treat you, the way we speak to you, isn't always kind. We have the best of intentions, but intent doesn't always matter. Not when your feelings are hurt."

"I'm stronger than you give me credit for."

"I know," I say softly. "But you're not stronger than *them*. You wouldn't stand a chance against a rogue vampire, and you know that. That's why we say what we say and do what we do. We aren't dismissing you as an invalid. We're just trying to keep you safe."

After everything I've been through, it takes a lot to surprise me, but Luna's reaction to my sympathy shocks me to my core.

She smiles. She smiles and shakes her head and diverts her gaze from mine. Something inside me shudders at the sight of this girl, a mortal in the midst of an immortal war, and when I tell her that she isn't strong enough to face an army that could cripple our nest, she *laughs*.

"I'm leaving now," she says.

"I'm going with you."

She doesn't respond. She simply shakes her head as she walks backward toward the tree line.

"I don't need protection," she says again, mirroring her words from earlier.

I want to argue, to tell her she's being ridiculous. Her pride is making her decisions, not her mind, but I can't speak. I am silenced by the unwavering sensation that cripples me.

We are not alone.

All at once, my skin feels as though it's on fire. The tiny hairs on my arms tingle, standing on edge. The sensation is a lot like fear. It bubbles in my chest, bursting my innards, and I am completely incapable of stopping it. At its mercy, I feel each rupture, each piercing cry as I am nuked from the inside.

I wonder how long spirit has been warning me. Ever since I transitioned into a vampire, I've used my magic less and less. I've smothered the witch without even realizing it. And now she's angry, but it isn't her wrath I fear most.

Luna is facing me. Her eyes are so wide, so bright white with terror, I almost believe she senses it too. But that's not possible. She's human. Her senses die off after five. And right now, my sixth sense is rapid firing at brain-melting levels.

Her back is to the forest, and despite the fact that it's daytime, the world is cloaked in darkness. The eclipse burns brightly over us but offers little light to extinguish the shadows.

Time moves so slowly, I think I can actually *hear* it ticking by, like the world is a clock and we're just slowly rotating in place until death.

I see the exact moment it happens, and I watch the realization settle over Luna's face as she too comes to the same conclusion.

She will be taken.

Like Jasik, Luna will fall victim to my father's war.

At first, I see his hands. One wraps around her waist and

pulls her backward until she is flush against his body. The other is wrapped around her throat, muffling her cries. She whimpers so softly, I worry her fear won't reach the ears of my allies inside the manor.

His thumb is resting against the throbbing vein in her neck as her overworked heart struggles to pump blood to her agitated body. The resounding thump against his skin is bliss. I know this even without speaking to him. At my darkest moment, when the vampire was so unhinged it considered the blood of an innocent, I felt that same thrill.

He smiles, baring teeth that are stained light pink from years of bloodshed, and he chuckles, the sound reverberating through his torso and into the soil beneath his bare feet. He wears no shirt, only pants. His jeans have been cut off at his shins, and they are torn in slashes. My hands tingle at the sight of them, and somehow, I just *know* the rips in fabric are from nails, from innocents desperate to get away.

His skin is stark white, and his arms are thin and bony. He yanks Luna to the side, and she yelps at the sudden jerk. When he does this, I notice his rib cage is prominently displayed, and I wonder if hunger is the reason he so blindly follows my father. Perhaps my father made him this way. Maybe, when they first met, this was a man—a kind, healthy man who became a beast only after enduring my father's torment.

Even though I try to stay focused on the rogue vampire before me, I can't help but think of another. There are pieces of my mind that trickle to Jasik, to the torture he is undoubtedly experiencing simply because he loved me. In the better part of a thousand years, he's made only one mistake: saving me.

"Ava," Luna says, her voice a desperate choke of muffled sounds.

The rogue moves his hand from her throat to her mouth, and he breathes into her ear, blowing so softly, loose strands of her hair flutter forward.

"Shh," he whispers, and Luna squeezes her eyes shut.

I take a single step forward, and the rogue *tsks* at me like I'm a child. Favoring his grasp on Luna's neck to waving a disapproving finger, he simply uses his tongue to express himself, and the sound of his *tsk* echoes all around us.

I stop in my tracks and scan the surroundings.

"I'm not alone," he says in an eerie, singsong voice.

He laughs again, the chuckle deep and childlike.

He is humming now, swaying side to side, and Luna moves with him. A single tear drips down her face and coats his hand where it still covers her mouth. He inhales deeply, succumbing to the euphoric ecstasy that is Luna's fear.

I see only the whites as his crimson irises roll to the back of his head, and I cringe when he swipes his tongue across her cheek, tasting her salty tears.

She screams, and even though it is muffled by his hand, the sound is loud enough to penetrate the walls of the manor and silence the arguing inside. Luna and I managed to walk clear across the garden. We now stand at the woods that surround our property, and even though the distance can easily be scaled by the hunters inside, it offers a solid head start to the rogue vampire, who is even faster.

His eyes flicker to the sight behind me. I don't have to turn around to know the hunters are approaching us. Soon they'll be at my side, and even if he isn't alone, we'll take them. We have to. We have to save her. We can't lose anyone else.

When he looks at me, his grin turns sinister, as though we've played right into his plan.

"Catch me if you can," he whispers.

And with that, he's gone. I blink, and he disappears into the forest, taking Luna with him.

# ELEVEN

We need to move quickly if we hope to rescue Luna, but I am frozen in place. Worming its way through shoe leather and cotton socks, the earth summons me. I feel its pull at the soles of my feet, and the entrapment is as strong as a riptide. I know I am standing on land, but my body feels weighed down, my muscles loose, as I am lost to the depths.

Luna doesn't feel the weight of my heavy limbs or the uncertainty of my mind, so she calls out to me, beckoning me to save her. Her voice is strained, her tone shattered. She shrieks as she says my name, screams as she begs for her release. I know she is crying even though I can't see her anymore.

The steady thump of hurried footsteps swirls within the darkness, twirling around me like a ribbon ... or a noose.

The sound comes from all around me. From behind. From my sides. Even from the distance, where Luna fights for her life against a threat she could never escape. Not without help. Not without us.

My gaze is glued to the forest, to the very spot Luna just stood. I can still feel her essence, smell her sweet aroma. The heat from her body lingers long after she is gone.

I blink, and Malik is standing in front of me, blocking my view. I do not move to look around him, because I know she is not there. So I close my eyes, inhaling deeply, and I smell her.

I don't stop pretending she's still here until Malik shakes me awake.

I yank free from his grip, stumbling backward, freed from the earth's mighty grasp.

"They *took* her," I hiss.

Malik ushers me to calm down, but I am seething. Every step he takes toward me, I take two more backward. The last thing I want to do is harm my leader when my frustration already has a target.

I whip around to find it, coming face-to-face with Jeremiah. He is a few feet away from me, standing near Holland, and I can't help but snort at the sight of them. It wasn't so long ago that *I* was accused of being childish because I cared more about rescuing Jasik than anything else.

"They took her because *you* didn't do your *fucking* job," I shout, pointing an accusatory finger in his direction.

My words escape me before I can process what I'm saying, and even I gasp at my tone. Every word I speak is icy and sharp. Jeremiah winces before trying to cover up the fact that I have wounded him with words alone. But he fails. His eyes betray his pain. A mortal is in danger because of his foolishness, and as a vampire, that's not an easy cross to bear.

He has an eternity to live with his bad choices, and if I were a better person, I wouldn't stoke the fire. I'd end his torment. But I'm not a good person. I'm too *angry* to be good. So not only will I stoke this fire—I will watch it burn.

"This one's on you," I say. "Remember that. We lost her because your loyalty can be so easily broken by a childhood crush."

I hate him, and I can't help that I do. My anger has control over me now, and even though I sense my downward spiral,

I can't stop it. I am pissed off at the world. At everyone and everything. We *knew* better. We knew Luna wasn't safe with us, and we let her stay anyway. We should have forced Jeremiah to patrol when we caught him skipping. Instead, we succumbed to petty fights about a future that won't exist if we don't stop my father. We've lost Jasik, most of the coven, and now Luna. Next on the list: our lives.

A hand rests on my shoulder, and I don't have to look up to know it belongs to Malik. His aura is so eerily similar to his brother's that I've been finding myself hopeful Jasik will be standing beside me. But when I turn, he's never there.

"We have to save her," I whisper to him.

"We will," he says. "We'll save them all."

I nod as I close my eyes to steady my rapid heartbeat. In the distance, I can still hear Luna. Her cries are muffled, and I fear the worst. When I inhale, her scent is scattered. It's as though she's everywhere all at once, and I know this is a parlor trick by the rogue vampire to throw us off their trail.

"Let's go," Malik says.

No longer soft and compassionate, his voice is stern, his words deliberate. This is an order to his nest from their leader.

As he speaks, he releases my shoulder, and I open my eyes to see Hikari trudge toward us. Her eyes are glued to Jeremiah, who teeters on his feet. He is torn between aiding his nestmates or staying with his boyfriend.

Malik doesn't need to explain to Jeremiah that he's at a crossroads. His decision today will determine his fate tomorrow. A vampire nest works similarly to a witch coven. We have a leader, we have orders, and we have a duty to our nest. Jeremiah is failing miserably in every possible way.

"Are you coming?" Malik asks.

But he doesn't wait for an answer. He has already turned his back on the vampire, the witches, and the manor beyond them.

As Malik walks into the forest, gliding past the tree line, I struggle to keep up with his long strides. Hikari is beside me, and she offers a sad smile when I look her way. I can tell she's as unsure as I am about the fate of our nest. I think we can all agree we lost the fight the night Amicia died. Despite our desperation to keep her legacy intact, some of the vampires left that very night, and the rest followed shortly after. What was once a bustling, thriving house is now creaky and desolate. The silence is almost unbearable. It looms like a threat, like a cautionary tale of how not to lead a vampire nest.

I don't think Malik is a particularly bad leader, even though I'm sure he'd disagree with me. None of this is his fault—not Amicia's death, Jasik's disappearance, or Jeremiah's tantrum. And it's not his fault Luna was taken.

"Blood," Hikari says.

Malik kneels down, lifting the broken branch to his nose, and inhales deeply. He shudders, and I know it's Luna's blood. Her essence has that effect on me too.

"She's leaving us a trail," I say.

"I'm surprised she'd take the risk," Hikari says.

"She knows she doesn't have much time."

"She's putting herself in greater danger."

"She isn't exactly trained for this, Hikari," I remind her. "She's mortal. She didn't grow up in this world."

Hikari snorts.

"Humans are obsessed with the undead," she says. "Vampires dominate popular culture. She knows more than she realizes."

Choosing to ignore our bickering, Malik stands and scans our surroundings. He inhales deeply, loudly, and I find myself doing the same.

"Over there," Malik says.

"All I'm saying is, it doesn't take a genius to know bleeding around vampires isn't a good idea," Hikari says. "The chances he hasn't already smelled her blood and—"

"Enough!" Malik shouts. "Stop talking, and act like hunters."

He's facing us now, and we both cower under his glare. I see the disappointment in his eyes, and it makes me squirm. I feel like I'm eight years old, and I've just been scolded by my mother for sneaking downstairs after bedtime to snack on her secret cookie stash.

"Sorry," Hikari says as she crosses her arms, but her bitter tone tells me she doesn't mean it.

"Rescuing her won't be easy," Malik reminds us. "Let's not make it harder on us by alerting him to our location."

I swallow hard and nod.

Malik turns away from us, and I risk a sideways glance to Hikari. Usually, she's all business, minimal bickering, but I think the stress of our situation is getting to her. I forget that I'm not the only one who's lost someone. Amicia was her sire. She meant to her what Jasik means to me. And her death created a domino effect that we may never recover from.

We sprint to the next location, stopping only a few meters from where we last stood. The scent of Luna's blood hangs heavy in the air. I taste it when I lick my lips. I taste her fear too. Hikari is right. She doesn't have much time.

A flash of movement at my side halts me. The others are too distracted by Luna's blood spill to notice. But I do.

Someone rushes through the brush as I slide my dagger from its sheath. I dash to meet him just as he exits the trees. My blade makes contact with his jacket, but I am stopped before I can plunge my weapon into his chest.

Jeremiah stares back at me, his hand gripping my wrist painfully hard. His eyes are wide, his breathing hitched. He came close—too close.

The tension in my muscles releases as I step backward, and he lets go of my hand. I sheath my weapon as my breathing begins to slow.

"Jer?" Hikari asks.

"You came," Malik says.

There is a drastic difference in tone between the two vampires. Hikari's voice is whisper soft, and her fear about what could have been is evident. Had Jeremiah not anticipated my response, he wouldn't have stopped my blade. He'd be dead right now.

Hikari may be ruled by her emotions, but Malik is not. His voice is calm, never wavering. He speaks plainly, pointedly, but the matter-of-fact tone he adopts doesn't fool me. He's as happy as I am to see Jeremiah. We need all the help we can get.

"Where's Holland?" Hikari asks.

I glance behind Jeremiah and stare into the dark distance. Much of my view is blocked by trees, but the shadows are stagnant. If Holland is there, he isn't moving.

"He stayed behind with the others," Jeremiah says.

"Is he working on the ritual?" Malik asks.

Jeremiah nods. "He says it won't be long now."

His words wash over me, blanketing me in a sense of security I desperately needed. The rush of my breath, the rapid beats of my heart, makes even my bones tingle with excitement. We might actually win this thing.

"But there aren't enough witches," Hikari says.

"And there will be one less human if we don't keep going," I say.

My words have more attitude than I intended, but my pointed remark gets the job done. Frivolous conversations cease, and we remember the real reason we're out here.

Silently, we track Luna by using the droplets of smeared blood she left behind. I try to remain focused, but my mind wanders to Holland and the remaining witches. He was confident his plan would work *before* we lost the coven. Now, with only the stragglers left, he's still sure.

I hate to worry, especially when we really could use some good news, but I can't help replaying the look in Jeremiah's eyes when he asked Holland to run away with him. Are we risking everything by trusting them? If they abandon us at the last minute and all our hope lies with Holland's plan, we're doomed.

I am halted by a shriek. Even without seeing her, I know it came from Luna. The air hums with each ragged breath she takes. It grows louder as she runs closer. The soil beneath my feet is radiated by shock waves with every step she takes, and I prepare myself for what's darting in our direction—just in case Luna isn't alone.

The overgrown evergreen blocking my view rustles, and a figure leaps out from the shadows. I hesitate a second longer than I normally do, ensuring I don't make the same mistake I made when I attacked Jeremiah, and I am greeted by Luna's wide, teary eyes.

She loses her footing when she sees me, screeching as she tumbles to the ground, breaking her fall with her hands. On her knees, she looks up at me and begins to cry.

I crouch beside her, wrapping an arm around her small, shivering frame, but I keep my eyes on the woods behind her. In my free hand, I hold my dagger in a white-knuckled grip. My arm is at my side, my clenched fist kept out of Luna's sight so I don't risk accidentally harming her with a sharp blade meant to slice through immortal bones.

Luna holds me tightly, her soft body melting into my more rigid frame. I can practically feel her fear subsiding as I comfort her. Like a succubus, she feeds on my strength, and for the briefest moment, my vigor wavers.

"How did you escape?" Malik asks, eyes narrowing as he assesses the girl.

"He—He l-let me g-go," she says.

She is distraught, stuttering as she speaks. Her words are broken by her tears, and each dramatic inhalation is like a knife to my heart. I put her in this situation when I befriended her, never thinking about the dire consequences my naïvety could have.

"He just . . . let you go?" Hikari asks.

Her tone is steeped in distrust, and I don't blame her. Luna's escape is spectacularly suspicious and makes zero sense. Even if the rogue vampire only took Luna to taunt us, he'd surely still kill her. Food is food, and rogues are driven by their bloodlust. It's what makes them different and dangerous.

"He s-said you'd f-follow me," she says.

Luna pulls away from my embrace and wipes under her eyes with her fingers, leaving streaks of dirt and blood spatter. Together with her tears, it looks like war paint, and I am reminded that we may have gotten Luna back relatively unharmed, but the battle is not over. There are still rogues to kill, humans to save, a world to make better.

"You came for me," she whispers.

I frown, wondering what I could have done to make her think the alternative was an option. Despite not knowing each other for very long, I've become quite attached to Luna. I suppose that's what happens when you make a new friend while surrounded by enemies. You grow close quickly.

But the longer I stay quiet, the more I think about what she said, the way she said it.

You came for me.

You came . . .

I'm here. Nearly alone. In the middle of the woods. During an eclipse. In a town infested with rogues.

He let her go.

I think about how strange Luna was acting when she showed up at the manor. She and Malik seemed transfixed. Their infatuation is still there, with each making sideways glances at each other when they think no one is looking. And once again, I am overwhelmed by my doubt. This isn't the first time my father planted a spy in our lives, and now that I know what he's capable of—and how far he'll go to get what he wants—my trust in others is quickly dissipating. I'm beginning to think the only person I can trust is myself.

"Why did he let you go?" I ask.

I swallow hard, stilling my body as I consider Luna's sudden appearance in my life. My gaze is fixated on her. I take it all in. Every line, every pore, every blemish, every crack in her dry lips. I stare into her eyes. I watch the way her pupils dilate as I lean toward her, desperate for her response.

Her heartbeat intensifies, and I listen to it as she responds, holding my breath for any hint of dishonesty.

*Thump. Thump. Thump.*

"Because you followed me here," she says, repeating herself.

"And why is that important?"

"You should have let him kill me," she says softly.

*Thump. Thump. Thump.*

Her heartbeat remains steady. No lie detected.

"There are more," she hisses.

Her voice is shaky, her breath unsteady, and tears begin to fall again. She sniffles loudly and wipes her nose.

Luna slouches as she rests her bottom on the heels of her feet. With her eyes closed, she pouts and fails to steady her emotions.

I remind myself that her reaction is understandable for a human thrown into a war between vampires and rogues. She doesn't seem to be lying to me. Maybe I am overreacting.

"There are too many," she says. "I couldn't fight that many. I had to run. I had to leave them behind."

She zones out as she rambles. I can tell her vision is distant by the clouded look of her eyes. She isn't seeing me, but she is seeing *something*. Since I'm not a mind reader, I focus on her confession. It displaces any fear I had that she might not be a true ally. I believe her. I believe *in* her. I don't know why I doubted her loyalty.

For what feels like centuries, Jasik has been with my father, and I haven't once worried that he may switch sides. But he can. At any minute, he can choose to turn rogue. To essentially turn off his emotional attachment to me, to us, and relish in his bloodlust. But he knows that's what my father wants. He wants to break him, so he'll fight back until his dying breath. I'm certain of this, so why am I so quick to judge the others?

I reach for Luna, rubbing my thumb against her quivering jaw. She opens her eyes when I make the connection, and I offer a weak smile.

"They're in Darkhaven, Ava."

She inhales sharply through her nose. The slurping sound her snot makes causes me to squirm. I drop my arm, but I don't move away from her. Not until she's ready and needs that amount of space. Right now, she's relying on my strength and protection, and I will give her what she needs.

"We have to go," I say to the others. "Humans stand no chance against them."

Malik is standing beside me, his towering frame shadowed by the eclipse above him. His features are masked, his face dark, his stance deadly, and instinctively, my innards clench. My body reacts this way whenever I'm in a position where I might be harmed. The vampire is more comfortable being predator, not prey.

But I don't move. Not until Luna's ready.

"You said there are more," Malik says. "How many more? Did you see them?"

Luna nods and digs her fingers into the dirt as she pushes herself up. She wobbles unsteadily on her feet and uses the back of her hand to wipe away the sweat at her temple. She looks so frail under the eclipse, like the phenomenon itself is making her weak.

"They look . . . different," she says.

"How?" I ask, but I already know the answer.

"Their skin is so pale," she says. "So much paler next to those lines. They look like veins, like blood veins, but they weren't blue. They were black."

I stand to face Malik fully. It's just as we feared. My father is farming amulets from the mines and using them to summon dark entities. I'm certain Sofía's behind this, and I chastise myself for being so stupid. I should have killed her the moment she came to Darkhaven.

That's a mistake I will never again make.

# TWELVE

We're in over our heads. It's what we're all thinking but too afraid to admit. Defeat isn't an option, but facing a rogue vampire army that's overpowered by demonic energy is suicide. Either way—we run or we stay—the odds aren't great.

"We should go back," Jeremiah says.

Coward.

While I understand his apprehension, we face near-death experiences all the time. It's in our job description. If we turn back now, we might as well call it quits, because we're not the heroes or saviors we think we are. Not if we allow rogue vampires to terrorize the humans of Darkhaven.

The fact is, even if we run, they'll eventually find us, and if we're going to die anyway, we might as well die with honor, protecting and fighting for what's right.

"Darkhaven needs us," Malik reminds him.

"It's time we face the facts," Jeremiah says. "They're stronger, faster, and far more intelligent than we've ever given them credit for."

"He's right," Hikari says. "We need to regroup, figure out what to do next."

"And in the meantime, we just let them treat Darkhaven as their personal smorgasbord?" I ask.

"No one is saying we *won't* help them," Hikari says. "We're just saying—"

"We're saying we need to protect our own first," Jeremiah says.

"Darkhaven *is* our *own*," I say. "This is *our* town. Those are *our* people. They need us. We can't turn our back on them now."

Luna shuffles awkwardly beside me. She shakes her head as she crosses her arms over her chest. She's pissed, and she doesn't hide it well. She's well aware that the terror she experienced is now being inflicted on Darkhaven. Those people were her friends, her neighbors, her customers. A death at the hands of rogue vampires is too cruel a punishment even for enemies.

"Let's be real here," Jeremiah says. "If those people knew the truth about us, about what we are, they would have driven us out long ago."

"Or worse," Hikari whispers.

"Humans are intolerant by nature," Jeremiah says. "Anything that strikes them as different is deemed evil or unnatural or *unworthy* of this life."

"He has a point, Ava," Hikari says. "I mean, humans can hardly get along with each other. We can't expect them to be on our side through this."

"They'll try to kill us even as we fight to save their lives," Jeremiah says.

"So you think it best to just abandon them altogether?" Malik asks.

"I'm just saying, we came for the girl," Jeremiah says. "Mission accomplished. Let's go home before we're hunted by rogues *and* humans."

"Is that what you think, Luna?" I ask. "I mean, you're human, yet you haven't once tried to kill us."

Luna looks away, gnawing on her lower lip and avoiding eye contact. I can't blame her for needing some space. She has just discovered the vampires responsible for protecting this town are weak, selfish pessimists. Even I'm embarrassed by their actions, and I would die for this town.

"I—I wouldn't. I mean, I . . . I don't want to hurt you," Luna says, stumbling over her words.

"She's an outlier to a much larger issue, and you know that," Jeremiah says. "Even your own blood tried to murder you. They nearly succeeded, too."

"And it's your father who's behind this," Hikari reminds me.

"Yet I still won't back down," I say. "I won't surrender, and I refuse to hand over Darkhaven to him."

"Your optimism is going to get us all killed," Jeremiah hisses.

"And your emotions are giving me whiplash, Jeremiah. And now you've roped Hikari into your schemes. I mean, where do you stand now? Are you on our side or not? Yes or no? Make up your mind, because if you're not going to help us, then just leave."

"I'm here, aren't I?"

"Barely."

"I *want* to help, but I don't want to die," he says. "We need to be smart about this."

"We have no intention of attacking blindly," Malik says. "With the help of the witches, we have a chance."

"But not if we keep bickering," I say. "It's exhausting, and we should be using what little time remains to our advantage."

"How can we do that?" Hikari asks. "From what Luna saw, I don't see how we can help them."

"We're not ready for a fight," Jeremiah says. "At least, not yet anyway. Holland needs more time."

"Well, he's out of time," Malik says. "There's nothing we can do about that. We will move forward with his plan and begin the ritual as soon as we return."

"Ava, what happens if we perform an incomplete ritual?" Jeremiah asks.

His tone is unmistakable. He knows exactly what will happen, as do the others. Performing an incomplete ritual is dangerous. Rituals involve summoning great forces of magic, and without a way to channel that power, the ritual itself will wreak havoc. To stop a rogue army, we intend to harness the power of the eclipse, one of the most powerful phenomena available to us. Even one small mistake can unleash more energy than the earth can handle, killing us all.

"The only thing that matters is the oath we made to protect this town," Malik says. "When we settled here, we promised we'd do whatever it took to keep the humans safe and the rogue population under control."

"Times were different then," Jeremiah says. "The human population has grown tenfold."

"We knew the world would change," Malik says. "We knew Darkhaven would grow, that more humans would settle here."

"But we were never overrun by rogues," Jeremiah whispers. "Not like this."

Jeremiah's voice cracks, betraying his true emotional state. He hides it well behind a wall of armor, each brick placed strategically to cover his fear. Like the rest of us, he's terrified, because the truth is, the enemy has taken control, and there are slim odds that we all make it out of this alive.

"There is always death in war," I say softly.

Since my transition, we've lost my former coven, including my mother and grandmother. My childhood best friend. Amicia. Will, the only other hybrid like me. And so many more. So many lives lost to a fruitless battle. Jeremiah is afraid he's next. And all he can think about are the missed moments with Holland, all the things he won't be here for if he dies. We share that fear. I'd give up everything I have to spend just one more day with Jasik.

"Make no mistake, we are at war," Malik says. "But unlike rogue vampires, we are honorable creatures. We will protect humans. We will fight until death."

"Let's hope it doesn't come to that," Jeremiah says.

"It will," Malik says. "If you wish to fight with us, you must be prepared to make the ultimate sacrifice."

Silence washes over us, clinging to the air like thick heat. It makes it hard to breathe, to think, to even speak. I want to say something uplifting, something that will make Jeremiah—and the others—see that everything will work out, that we will make it through this, that my father's army will fall, and we will live to see another day.

But even I can't lie that well.

The trees rustling in the distance catch my eye. There is a flash of something familiar—a torn shirt, pale skin, crimson eyes, the scent of blood and dust. My insides twist, my heart drops. And somehow, I know. I just . . . *know.*

My father is here.

And he's taunting me.

The sensation of being watched is something I can't easily shake. One of the first lessons I learned as a novice witch was to recognize those signs, because time was never in our favor. Not when we faced immortal threats. The vampires held all the power. They were faster, stronger, and better, more ruthless hunters, so we relied on our magical instincts—the way our skin prickled and pulse quickened, the pain from our clenched innards, the sound of spirit whispering in our ear, and the bitter taste as a slop of bile worked its way into our mouth.

Vampires brought out the worst in us.

Because of this training, I know we are being watched. It's him. I *know* it's him. I can *feel* it. Because my insides are screaming, and my skin is humming. There is a subtle shift in the air—the very one I am all too familiar with. When I focus on the darkness that surrounds us, I hear him. The sound of hurried breath and a rapid heartbeat causes the hunter within to buzz with excitement. The predator is awake, and she is ready for a fight.

Without thinking, I rush toward him, ready to end this once and for all. As my feet smack the ground, radiating shock waves up my legs, I think about all the times I've said that since I transitioned. How many times have I sworn that this would be the last time? How many times did I say I would end things . . . tonight?

I scoff at that girl. That naïve, innocent girl. She frustrates me now. I was too eager, ready to prove myself worthy of a truce no matter the cost, but I had no idea my own father was orchestrating my demise. Without him, I may finally know real, true, honest peace.

The sound of my name echoes in the distance. One by one, my friends shout for me, but I ignore them. I focus solely on my father. His voice, raspy and deep, draws me to him, summoning me like the night sky calls to the moon, and I listen, like a werewolf hexed.

His siren call leads me to the edge of the forest, and as I peer past the trees, gazing at Main Street, I am halted by what I see, frozen in place. Because I dreamed this before. This is a scene from a nightmare that forever haunts me.

A river of crimson flows down the pavement, spilling onto the toes of my boots. The air is stifling. It's thick and still. The scent of blood is heavy in my lungs, and when I am finally graced with a calm breeze, the hot, sticky air only makes my stomach churn.

Everything before me has been tainted by magic—the air and the earth beneath it are too raw, too vulnerable to be mundane. There was too much. Too much too quickly. Too much in one place. With nowhere to go. It causes my pulse to race, so I clutch my chest, fearful my heart might burst free from its shackles, joining the heaping, bloody mound before me.

My head is spinning as leftover magic reaches out to me, desperate for a host. It mistakes me for the earth, its true home, where all untethered magic recedes when our earthly forms die. It's as though the magic has taken on a life of its own, because the moment it recognizes my body as capable of carrying the weight of elemental control, it calls to me. The air was already warmed by its presence, but now it crackles.

Untamed magic is extremely dangerous, and I've just put myself in its path.

Even though I know this—I *know* I cannot consume this magic as my own without being ripped apart—I cannot move. My arms hang heavily at my sides as I teeter on my feet, swaying as bile burns in my gut, desperate for an escape. I drool—desperate to swallow, unable to do so, and feeling every second as a stream of spit worms its way down my chin.

I want to scream. I want to shout at the earth to fulfill its duty, to claim this leftover magic as its own. But there is just so much, too much, and it's *everywhere*. It's in the trees and the rocks. It's in the soil and the air. And it's in the mound of dead bodies piled up only a few feet from where I stand.

They mock me. I may have life—for now—but I too am unable to control my limbs.

My anger is beginning to take control, and I welcome it. With a clear head, I may not free myself before it's too late. But when ruled by my emotions, I am rash, reckless, and maybe that's the only way I can escape. If a host offers unfavorable conditions, the parasite won't survive. And that's what this magic is. Anything not meant as mine is parasitic.

I need to focus, to wake up. This isn't my nightmare anymore.

I start small and clench my fists, pumping them open and closed. This little movement takes all my effort, but I can feel my hardened muscles loosening.

I swallow what's spilled into my mouth, focusing on the sour taste of uncertainty. I scan my surroundings, praying my friends find me before a rogue vampire does. Thankfully, I am alone and still somewhat camouflaged by the trees.

I'm sweating heavily now—courtesy of both uncontrolled magic and bodily strain. I shudder as each streak drips down my forehead, tickling exposed skin.

I ball my hand into a fist and smack my leg to wake my muscles. I'm not sure if this will work, but I am surrounded by magic, and as it begins to seep its way into my body, this is my only option.

It's stronger now. I can feel it as the air brushes against

my skin. It stings and pierces, clawing its way inside a host not meant for this much magic. It takes everything I have to fight back, to slow its progression into my body.

The river of blood has reached the tree line, and my boots are sinking into the soggy earth that's rich with bloodshed. I inhale deeply, lungs shaking. I try to call for Malik, for anyone, but my voice betrays me.

The bloodbath before me catches my attention once again, and I focus on it. For a split second, it's all I can see. Mangled bodies scream at me with the desperation of stifled pleas—limbs torn from torso, throats ripped apart, skin stained with tears. And blood. It's *everywhere*. Like the magic they left behind, the blood coats everything and everyone.

But their eyes. Their eyes are lifeless. Blank, devoid pits. I squeeze mine shut, not wanting to see it anymore.

They left because they were afraid. They left because they thought their efforts were better spent protecting the humans of Darkhaven.

He knew.

Like always, he was watching us.

And they were ambushed.

My father was listening. He's *always* listening. He is always one step ahead.

And now they're dead, and I'm spinning. I can *see* each crack in my sanity as I keep my eyes shut. We might not have been allies, but I swore to protect these people. I failed them. I failed everyone.

My father is winning this war, and he knows it. He knows the witches of Darkhaven were our best chance at beating him, so he murdered them all, and he left them on display for all to see.

# THIRTEEN

The steady pounding of hastening footsteps echoes in my mind. Someone is approaching from behind, and they're swarming fast. The earth buzzes, radiating a sound eerily similar to that of cicadas in the summertime, and all I can do is wait. Wait and listen.

I blink, and the blurred figure of Malik is before me. He's arrived so quickly, my exhausted senses can barely keep up. His mouth is moving, and I think he's speaking, but I hear nothing. Nothing but an ear-piercing screech that comes at me from all sides.

The painful strain on my stiffened muscles is all I can think about, and as I sink farther into the soggy earth, I worry my last memories, before I'm buried alive, will be of the almost dozen dead and dismembered witches. They died fighting, with their eyes open, and those lifeless pits stare back at me, accusatory and judgmental.

Malik grabs my arms, squeezing them so hard I worry the last sound I'll hear before I succumb to a magical prison is my bones breaking under the pressure. My fear must play across my face, because he loosens his grip on me, but he never lets go.

I shut my eyes, willing myself to turn off all senses, but this never works. As much as I relish the idea of an emotionless state, I'd be no better than a rogue vampire, hellbent on sating my bloodlust alone. And I refuse to stoop to their level.

So I still hear it. Still feel it.

The magic from nearly an entire coven was released the moment they died, and I stumbled upon it too quickly, too soon after it was forced from its earthly restraints. Now it's free. It should have found sanctuary in the earth. But it refuses to retreat. Because I'm here, and I'm a vessel. Why dissipate when you could live on . . . *forever*? A hybrid is an awfully good host, and magic is far from ignorant of that fact.

"What's wrong with her?" Hikari asks.

My eyes are still shut, so I focus on her voice. It's strained by her worry. Perhaps I look worse than I feel. Or maybe I appear as though nothing is wrong, and all they see is an unmoving, unblinking, unspeaking hybrid.

I know I should explain, but I'm not sure I have the strength to form the words they need to hear. They're vampires. They'll never understand how this feels. They'll never be in this kind of danger. Because magic will never seek asylum within the dead.

"Ava?" Luna says.

I suck in a sharp breath at the sound of her voice, flinching as she walks nearer to me. Her footsteps are slow and intentional, and she speaks softly, as to not startle me.

Maybe she understands. She's catered to the witches of Darkhaven at Lunar Magic for years. Maybe she can explain to the others that the moment I stop fighting this magic is the moment I'll lose control. And that can't happen again. I refuse to fall victim to another force that only wishes to use my body for its own agenda.

Luna touches me, brushing her fingertips against my

balled fist, and I wince at the sensation.

I'm used to her drawing emotions from me that are new and unexplainable. Everything from her scent to her sound pleases the vampire inside, but that's not a problem when I have control. But right now, I can't fight the vampire, and she's too close. Dangerously close. She sees her friend in trouble when she should see an immortal on the brink of a power boost.

"It's everywhere," I whisper through clenched teeth, hoping she will understand.

I use my thoughts to will it away, to put distance between the energy eruption and me, but all I can do is think about how it feels. Magic assaults every inch of my body. It is a parasite that's skittering against my skin, desperate for a way in, and the sensation to scratch until I bare raw flesh is almost too much to ignore.

It feels like it's in my head, worming and crawling through my brain, devouring every memory, every reaction, every emotion that makes me . . . *me*. I just want to scream and rip out my hair and tear off my skin until I can pull each and every magical leech from my body.

I begin to shake from the strain I've put on my muscles, and it takes every ounce of willpower I have not to collapse. I refuse to fall victim to the very magic I was born with, magic I trained with, magic I wielded to protect the people of this town, offering my very life when I failed.

"We need to leave," Jeremiah says. "Now. We need to get her out of here."

"Do you know what's wrong with her?" Malik asks.

"Holland warned me that this would happen," he says.

"*What* would happen?" Malik asks.

"There's too much magic," he says. "Holland explained

that when a witch dies, their magic is released, because magic never dies."

"Yes, that's right," Luna says. "Vampires might claim to be immortal beings, but the only thing that never truly dies is magic. It just...passes on."

"To what?" Hikari asks.

"Another host," Luna says.

I can feel their eyes on me, scanning every inch of my body. I'm already under attack, so adding another layer to this assault only enhances the panic and desperation I feel. I wish they would look away, would leave me alone. Better yet, I wish they'd take Jeremiah's advice and get us the hell out of here.

"From my research, covens are supposed to handle the transfer of power," Luna says.

"What happens when there isn't a coven left to do that?" Hikari asks.

"The earth absorbs it," Jeremiah says.

"Why isn't that happening?" Malik asks.

"Maybe her father did something to prevent it?" Hikari asks. "I mean, he killed his former coven, right? The fire? And he did something there too."

"We're talking about a lot of magic," Luna says. "That would take more power than he should have access to."

"Well, of course," Hikari says. She sighs heavily, dramatically, and chuckles before continuing. "I mean, that's on par with how things have gone lately, right? Let's imagine the worst-case scenario and then double it. Those tend to be our odds."

"I'm not so sure he's actually done anything," Luna says. "The reason a coven gets involved is because earth absorption is a slow process. These witches just died. Literally just died. Their magic is—"

"Everywhere," Malik says softly.

"And from what Holland has told me, that's not a good thing for nearby witches," Jeremiah says.

"It's looking for a host," Luna says.

"And it found one," Malik says. "It wants inside her."

"I'm guessing it's already trying," Luna says.

"That's why she can't move?" Hikari says. "Or . . . open her eyes? Blink?"

"The magic from one witch would be doable," Luna says. "But the magic from an entire coven? This many witches?"

"What will happen?" Malik says.

"She'll . . . die."

"This is crazy," Hikari says. "I don't feel anything."

"You wouldn't," Jeremiah says. "You're not a witch."

"But I'm a vampire, with heightened senses. Surely, I'd feel—"

"You'd feel nothing, Hikari," Luna says. "You're a vampire. You're not magical. You're just . . . dead."

Hikari snorts, and I can practically feel her annoyance radiating off her body. It's yet another layer added to the already overwhelming wave pulling me down. I'm nearly submerged within this magical riptide, and with each passing second, it's harder to breathe, harder to think, harder to just . . . stay afloat.

"Holland worried this would happen during the ritual," Jeremiah says. "If too many died too quickly, and we were all distracted by a rogue army—"

"We're leaving," Malik says.

"What about them?" Hikari asks. "Shouldn't we clean up this mess? The humans will surely notice a pile of dead bodies."

"They'll blame the wolves," Luna says. "They always blame the wolves."

"Ava," Malik whispers.

I need him to understand the severity of this situation, that everything Luna and Jeremiah are saying is true. If we don't get out of here, I'll lose this fight. I may be strong, but I don't stand a chance against chaotic, angry energy expelled too soon from its host.

I can tell from the tone of his voice that he's standing only a few inches from me, so I risk everything and open my eyes. My lip quivers as a tear escapes, and I focus on the sensation as it cascades down my cheek. I have to. I have to think only about the little things, the tiny moments that keep me in control.

Malik frowns at me and cups my face in his hand. He rubs away the tear with his thumb, and I do not shy away. His touch feels nothing like Luna's. Hers felt like a fiery invasion, whereas Malik's skin is cool, like mine. I lean against him, needing to feel his trademark stoicism before I crumble into the abyss, and he must recognize this desire, because he holds me carefully.

"I'm going to lift you now," he whispers.

His breath is cool against my temple, and as he speaks, I feel his lips brush against my skin.

With one hand at my back and the other behind my knees, he lifts me into his arms. I fall against him, relishing in his superior strength. Even though the thought leaves me guilt ridden, I can't help but wish I were a succubus. Absorbing his energy to replace what's been depleted would make me feel a lot better right about now.

Malik smiles down at me as I am cradled against his body, and for the smallest of seconds, I forget there's magic all around me. I forget the pain I feel as it forces its way into my body, and I forget that I'm slowly shutting down to escape it.

There is only him, only me. I've only ever felt this safe one other time—with Jasik.

If I close my eyes and focus on this feeling, I can trick myself into believing it is my sire who's cradling me now, not his brother. But I don't. I don't break his gaze. I stare into his crimson irises, and I let myself be happy...if only for a moment.

Their screams break my trance.

It is a sharp, painful screech that snaps me back to reality. Their outcry is the sound of true fear, and I've heard it so infrequently in my life that it stings my heart. A shudder works its way through my spine. I squirm in Malik's arms, but he only holds me tighter, refusing to let go.

Hikari cusses under her breath. She speaks so softly, I wonder if she actually said anything at all. Maybe it was the wind—the howling gust cursing this wretched night. But when she begins to back away slowly, eyes trained on something in the distance, I know it wasn't just a breeze.

I shift in Malik's embrace, scratching at his arms in a sad attempt to see what's behind us. I strain my neck, never quite reaching what lies just beyond. Understanding my concern, Malik turns slowly, offering me a full view of what has spooked the others.

I scan our surroundings, searching for the source. My gaze lands on the river of blood as it encroaches on the woods, dampening the soil so it too looks eerily black under the dimly lit sky.

I skim over the mound of dead bodies—all piled neatly

on display—and ignore the sinking feeling in my gut when I make eye contact with a dead witch. Like the others, she's still judging me.

I blink, and I see them. I suck in a sharp breath and choke out a cough as it catches in my throat. I am so loud, they make eye contact with me, and the terror in their eyes makes me wish I was still looking at dead witches.

Humans.

There are two. One man. One woman. They are standing a few yards away from the mound of dead bodies that will certainly be tied to us now. We may not have started this war, but the town will ensure that we face the consequences.

The woman is clinging to the man, digging her long nails into his jacket so tightly, the thread is beginning to tear. Her mouth is open, and she is still screaming.

The vampire in me is annoyed by her wail and wondering how long it will take until she has expelled all breath, silencing her screams. But the witch is angry—anger directed at my father for putting us in this situation, and anger at myself for allowing magic to be exposed. The internal war I experience as a hybrid—part vampire, part witch...or better yet, part predator, part prey—is utterly exhausting, especially tonight.

The man is holding on to her, arms wrapped tightly around her waist as he tries to steer them backward without taking his eyes off the scene before them.

I try to imagine what this might look like to someone inexperienced in the art of war. There are five of us—four vampires, one human. We are standing so close to the murder scene that our boots are steeped in blood.

But what likely shocks them more than the idea of encountering a mass murder scene and five possible serial killers is how different we must look. We're pale—*too pale*—especially next to Luna's darker complexion. And our crimson irises sparkle under the moonlight. There may be an eclipse overhead, but it certainly isn't dull enough to hide glowing eyes.

Would it be a far leap for them to assume we're vampires? After all, Hikari mentioned how humans are obsessed with the idea of an immortal life. They may have never met a vampire in person, but they have been bombarded with the idea of vampirism on both screen and page. Vampires are everywhere. Literally.

So even as I deduce that they are on to us and that there is no way we can talk our way out of this mess, I try not to panic. I have bigger things to worry about than this—like how every second I spend worrying about exposure, I am losing my battle against the magical assault on my body.

"I'll take care of them," Jeremiah says.

Even without explanation, I know exactly what he means. We all do.

Exposure is dangerous, and the witches of Salem learned long ago that humans cannot be trusted. So they left before the trials began and watched as innocents were convicted and murdered by their own people. There was nothing they could do, for if they stopped the trials, they'd out themselves. The war on magic would never end. So they walked away.

If we allow these humans to tell people what they saw, *who* they saw, we risk the same atrocities, and modernity would make escaping nearly impossible. Where can we go where there are no cameras, no phones, no televisions to spread false narratives about what it means to be a vampire or a witch?

To remain safely in the dark, to protect our secret,

Jeremiah is offering to do the one thing we swore we'd never do. He is going to kill humans.

We worked very hard to avoid this situation, and even though we've spent our lives fearing what some deem inevitable, we've never had a plan in place for what to do when Darkhaven discovers we are here. Already, they blame the wolves, slaughtering them by the dozens when they discover a rogue vampire attack victim. What will they do when they realize the monsters they seek take human form? They'll execute anyone they deem a vampire, even innocents.

But we're not monsters. We don't hide in the shadows because we want to. We shield ourselves from them because we have to, because human history is unkind to anyone who strays off society's planned path. We need to make them understand and trust us, like Luna has. And that's possible. She's proof of that.

"We can't," I whisper.

"We have to," Malik says.

Jeremiah walks toward them, closing the space quickly. The woman nearly trips over her heels, but the man holds her upright as they shuffle backward. Their eyes are wide, their breathing chaotic. The pounding of their hearts is only overshadowed by the constant buzzing in my ears.

The witches may be dead, but their magic has taken on a life of its own. And as a cohesive unit of elemental power, it's not happy that the choice we've made to protect our secret is to murder two humans.

"It's angry," I say.

I lick my lips, swiping at sweat, and struggle to keep my eyes open. I wince as my innards twist, and even though I know it's likely a sensation made up in my mind, I am absolutely certain I feel something rupture. This magic wants in, wants to use my body to correct our mistakes, and it will do whatever it needs to do to force me into submission.

So I do the only thing I can think of. I rely on Malik. I dig my fingers into his arm, and when his scent hits my senses, I focus on it.

The taste of his blood is the last thing I remember before everything goes black.

# FOURTEEN

I am awake before my eyes even open.

My lids are impossibly heavy, much like my limbs, and I am lying on something soft. I tease the fabric with my fingertips and realize I am no longer stranded in the forest, staring down at a pile of dead bodies or looking into the accusatory gazes of fearful humans.

I am home. I am safe.

I open my mouth to speak but only succeed in releasing a few painful huffs. Still, I try to call out to my friends, but the noises I make are never loud enough to catch the attention of anyone nearby. My lips are chapped and cracking, and my tongue sticks to the skin when I try to wet them.

My stomach growls so loudly it causes my body to shake. I assume my heightened healing abilities are spent, and I'll need to feed before another fight. Without a refuel, I won't survive. Our stock is critically low—or maybe even completely depleted—so this is yet another issue to contend with.

As happy as I am to be at the manor, I'm surprised I'm still alive. The last thing I remember is the smell of Malik's blood, but then everything went black. This isn't the first time I've lost consciousness while fighting this fruitless war, but this is the first time another coven's magic attempted to possess my body.

And it nearly succeeded.

I feel stiff and sore, and I'm not yet ready to see the world. So I breathe deeply, letting each inhalation soothe my achy body. My racing heart begins to steady, as do my devastating thoughts, and slowly, the vision of dead witches and terrorized humans fades away.

When I finally open my eyes, I am greeted by the sight of several witches staring down at me.

I furrow my brow at the sight. Instinctively, I retract, desperate to put space between us, but since I am lying on my back, there is nowhere to go. It makes me uncomfortable to have so many faces I don't know keeping their full attention on me.

Holding hands, they have encircled me.

I squint, blinking several times to clear the foggy haze, and when I can see them more clearly, I notice that even though their heads are tilted down at me, they aren't looking at me at all. Their eyes are glossed over, and they are chanting so softly, I can't hear their words.

With each passing second, I begin to feel better. The deep-rooted ache in my bones lessens, my innards untwist, my head stops racing, and I am no longer sweating as though the temperature in the room has reached one hundred degrees Fahrenheit. The air feels clearer now, less stuffy and sticky and gross. With the heat's absence, a cool breeze envelops me, and I welcome it with open arms.

I know the exact moment it's over. Not because their chants cease or they release their hands. Not because they step away in unison and offer me some much-needed space. Not because my friends rush over and ask if I'm okay. But because the wave of nausea I've felt since stumbling upon the mass grave is gone. The moment that magic dissipated, I was free.

"We have returned the magic to the earth," Holland says, mirroring my thoughts.

It takes a powerful witch to perform that ritual, especially when the magic involved isn't from his own coven, and now that it's over, I can see the toll it has taken on Holland.

With the back of his hand, he wipes away the sweat that has pooled at his forehead and offers me a weak smile. His eyes are sunken, tired, and I wonder how long it has been since he last slept. As I scan the room, I notice everyone looks a bit defeated.

"Where exactly did you send it?" Hikari asks.

As a vampire, she doesn't truly understand how this process works. Magic and covens and the elements are a bit too complex for someone not born into this world. She has a basic idea, but her knowledge is no greater than that of a human, who bases their ideas on information from scripted television shows and movies.

"We sent it where it should have gone to begin with," Aurelia says.

Hikari rolls her eyes at the canned response, and just for a moment, I want to laugh. I forget about the trauma we've endured, and everything feels as it should—with the witches as ambiguous as ever, the vampires distrusting of newcomers, and me in the middle just trying to keep the peace.

"I'm quite impressed you survived its attack long enough to reach us," Aurelia says to me.

"She's right," Holland says. "You're really lucky, Ava."

"She's strong," Aurelia says. "Like her mother."

The mention of my mother brings a smile to my face. I like to remember her that way. Strong, confident, fearless, ready to do whatever necessary for the good of her coven—or in my case, nest. I am eager for those images to replace the last memories I have. The ones where she ousts me from my home and then kidnapped me and forced rituals upon me to smother the vampire. Or the many, many times she tried to kill me. Those memories sting a bit.

"How do you feel?" Holland asks.

I think about his question before I answer. In all honesty, I feel pretty good. I feel as well as I did before I stumbled upon the aftermath. It's almost as if the attempted magical assassination never even happened.

"Better," I say.

As if on cue, a loud, steady growl erupts from beneath my shirt. I snort as I rub my stomach. I've learned that hunger means something different to vampires. It's a lot like a witch's magic, because it too can take on a life of its own, almost becoming a real-life entity. Rogues are driven by it, submitting to its every whim. It's what makes them so different from us. They've allowed their hunger to have a mind of its own, overriding rational thought to get what it wants: blood. Which is why if I want to stay in control, it's important that I feed when hungry.

"You're hungry," Luna says.

For a human without heightened senses, Luna has become spectacularly good at reading the room. I'm beginning to think it's her superpower, and maybe, just maybe, she's the bridge we need to eliminate the gap between mortals and immortals.

I gnaw on my lip as I think about that, about the humans of Darkhaven and how unprepared they are for this war. Maybe that's our fault. We chose to remain in the dark as a safety precaution, and in doing so, we've left them vulnerable.

Luna hands me a small container of blood. Mesmerized by the sloshing crimson liquid, I stare at it for a long time before I speak.

"I thought we were out," I say, gaze still glued to the plastic cup in my hands.

"I kept one hidden beneath the ice packs," Luna says.

"Why?" Hikari asks.

I can tell by her tone that she still doesn't trust Luna. At least not as much as I do. As much as I wish she did, I don't comment on it. If I've learned anything during my time with the vampires, it's that we need to trust gut reactions.

I didn't like Sofía from the start, and no one believed me when I said she was evil. Look where we are now. If we caught on to her plan sooner, Jasik might still be here. I might still have the amulet. Things could be so different if only they listened to me. So while I trust Luna completely, I won't ask the others to fall in line.

"Honestly, I wasn't sure if you'd have enough self-control to save some," Luna says. "Binge eating is a real problem, and I just knew something would happen, and we'd need one fast."

"And *just* how did you know that?" Hikari asks.

"Hikari," I say with a sigh.

"It's a fair question," Hikari answers. "You have to admit that it's suspicious when an outsider shows up with spare blood because they *just knew* we'd need it. We only need to feed this much after an attack."

"Common sense?" Luna says.

Hikari narrows her eyes at Luna, and I can tell she's reaching her breaking point. First the witches are vague as hell, and now Luna. After everything that's happened, it's a bit much for one vampire to accept, and even though Hikari's annoyance is justified, I don't want her anger to do something we'll all regret.

"You know, our situation is pretty dire," Luna says. "It just makes sense to save extra blood."

I shoot Hikari a look that silences her.

"Thank you," I say to Luna. "Once again, you've saved the day."

Luna beams brightly at the compliment, but after everything that's happened today, her radiance is a little too bright, so I have to look away.

I hang my legs over the side of the couch, and my boots smack against the hardwood louder than I intended. The room is silent now, with all eyes on me. But I'm not ready to look back at them, so I stare at my lap.

Slouching forward, I rest my elbows on my thighs, and in my hands, I am still holding the last remaining source of blood—the one every vampire in this room would love to have. Guilt washes over me because I know I will drink it. I have no other choice.

I toss the container between my hands, watching as the thick liquid sloshes within its clear prison. As it flows back and forth, over and over again, I am lulled into a memory—one I care never to relive.

When no one is speaking, the grandfather clock in the upstairs hallway ticks louder than usual, and that steady beat plays in unison with the sloshing inside this cup. Together, they sound ominous, like the eerie cackle of a nearby crow.

With nothing to distract me, it takes no time at all for me to see them in my mind's eye—their haunting gazes, their silenced pleas, their abrupt goodbyes. That river of blood flowing down the street, spilling into the forest, tainting the sacred earth. It's too similar to the blood offering in my hands.

"What happened to them?" I ask, speaking softly.

Even though I wish to never relive this night, to instead think up my own ending, one where the humans survived and we won, I need to know if Jeremiah killed those people. I need to know if we're no better than the rogue vampires we hunt.

"We let them go," Malik says to my surprise.

I meet his eyes, and even though dishonesty is a trait Malik finds unappealing, I search for proof of a lie. But I find none. My leader is looking back at me, standing tall, eyes focused. He does not blink or falter. His tone does not change. His heartbeat is steady.

I think I believe him. I think he really did let them go.

"It was the right choice," I whisper.

"We'll know soon enough," Jeremiah says.

"Nothing happened after I rescued that boy from the mines," I remind them.

"That was a child," Hikari says. "Kids make up stories to justify their trauma all the time. Adults are different."

"There are plenty of adults who believe and say crazy things," Luna says.

I smile at her, silently thanking her for coming to my defense—though I'm not surprised she did. If anyone would be against killing humans, it would be Luna and Holland. Both have lived with humans far longer than the hunters. Their connection to the outside world is different. The vampires think only of war and blood. The witches think only of the next generation and protection.

"They've encountered rogue vampire victims before," I say. "They blamed it on the wolves."

Luna frowns at this and shakes her head as she stares

at the floor. She crosses her arms over her chest, betraying her discomfort. No one else is looking at her, so no one else notices. But I do, and I realize this isn't the first time she's been bothered by talk of dead wolves. As a witch, I understand her frustration. Witches live in harmony with the earth, and needlessly killing her creatures used to upset me too.

"The reason those looked like animal attacks is because they were mauled and left behind, usually in the woods," Hikari says. "Group hunts do look like pack killings."

"This was different," Malik says. "Their remains were piled in the middle of Main Street. Animals wouldn't do that."

"The scene did look . . . *intentional*," Hikari says. "If I were a human investigator, I'd notice that it looks different from the bodies found in the woods."

"The witches will help cover it up," I say. "We used to spread lies to mislead the humans all the time."

"Except most of the witches are dead now," Jeremiah says.

I wince at this, looking away and trying not to think about everything this war has cost Darkhaven.

Jeremiah's right, but I don't want to admit it. There are only a few covens left, and even though they have no interest in helping us now—especially after the last two covens to help us were massacred—lying about what happened benefits them too. So even without asking, I know they'll do this for us.

History has proved that humans can't be trusted. Keeping them in the dark is as much for us as it is for them.

Without Jasik, our bedroom suite feels empty and hollow. I know he isn't here, but I can feel him. His essence, his scent—

it's everywhere. If I close my eyes, I can picture him standing beside me, arms wrapped around my waist, pulling me in for a kiss. But then I open my eyes, and he's not there. Despair is a painful, everlasting void.

I stare at my muddled reflection in the mirror and swipe away the fog. The cleared streak shows a small portion of my face at an awkward angle. Tears drip from my crimson eyes. I didn't even realize I was crying. I sniffle, pushing down the deep, overwhelming agony that rises in my chest, and continue cleaning off the glass with a towel.

I shiver as droplets of water cascade down my nude frame. I think I spent a good hour in the shower, scrubbing away the sweaty, bloody evidence of this terrible day. Seeing the water finally run clear didn't have the impact I was hoping for. I still feel icky and violated and exhausted. I still feel lost without him.

I yawn. The blood I consumed an hour ago didn't do much for my exhaustion, and it certainly didn't deter my cravings. I'm still hungry and ornery, and when I get hangry, I get reckless. I need to think straight and not make rash decisions. Recklessness will only get us killed.

I rush through my routine, pulling my hair back into a tight bun, and dress quickly. I opt for my usual all-black combat attire and slide on my boots. I cleaned them before I showered, but the scuffs in the leather will never go away. They are a constant reminder of everything I've fought for and everything I lost.

When I exit the bathroom, I am halted. Luna is sitting on the edge of my bed. Her hands are in her lap, and she is nervously fidgeting with her nails. Her rapid heartbeat overpowers the clicking noise her tongue is making as she tries to fill the silence.

Her gaze meets mine. She smiles, but it doesn't reach her eyes. Her apprehension is evident in her jittery quirks, but when I look into her eyes, I am surprised to see fear. I'm not sure if she's afraid because she's alone with me or because it's clear she has something to say that I might not like to hear.

I brace myself, preparing for the worst.

"Thank you for trying to protect those people," Luna says.

I relax, grateful this is nothing more than a semifriendly visit. The last thing I need right now is more devastating news.

Perhaps she's still upset about being kidnapped and nearly killed. Or maybe stumbling upon a bloodbath has her on edge—one she would have been part of if we hadn't found her in time. She's human, after all. That experience would cause any mortal to be a bit agitated and squirmy.

Maybe I'm just reading too much into this. With all the betrayals coming at me, I'm relying too heavily on body language to determine everyone's inner thoughts.

"I know standing up to your friends can't be easy," she says.

"It's not. But it was the right thing to do. Those people didn't deserve to die just because we messed up."

"You're honorable ... for a vampire," she says, mumbling the last part, but my heightened hearing picks up every word.

Something is different. Her tone isn't quite the same, and I rarely see her so nervous that she frets like this. She is staring at the floor again, kicking her legs back and forth where they dangle over the edge of my bed, and her heartbeat has yet to slow to a normal pace.

"Are you scared that they'll tell people about you?" she asks.

I shrug, trying to play it cool but failing miserably.

In all honesty, I am petrified that word will spread and the world will fall into old habits. I worry about humans attempting to hunt creatures they couldn't possibly beat. I worry I'll wake up one day, and the manor will be set on fire during daylight hours. I worry about the innocents—the ones who are deemed evil even though they aren't one of us. It will be humanity that faces the consequences of our existence if they discover we are here.

But I don't say any of this, because I need Luna to believe I'm stronger than I am.

"A little," I admit. "But my fear of the unknown doesn't give me the right to play God with innocent lives."

If only humans thought that way...

Luna smiles and meets my gaze, and I realize I'm coming off a bit preachy. I may sound righteous now, but I'm no angel. I've done bad things too, and I will spend the rest of my life repenting for my sins. I'd just rather not add more lives to my death list.

I cross the room until I'm only a few feet from her.

I like the way she smells. Her aroma is sweet and subtle—so much so, I think only vampires feel this way around her. She makes my pulse race and mind fog. I lick my lips as I stare at the throbbing vein in her neck. The longer we sit in silence, the greater my desire grows. The air between us has become intimate.

She swallows hard, and I realize I'm hyperfocusing and making her nervous.

To distract me from my hunger, I clench my jaw shut and sit on the bed beside her. I stare at the doorway to the bathroom, willing myself to go back in time and start this over again—hopefully in a less creepy manner.

I feel the pull of her at my side, so I fill the void with conversation.

"Is there something you want to tell me?" I ask.

She swallows again, and for a brief moment, all I can think about is the squishing sound in her esophagus. The air is hot now, too hot, *magically hot*. I know it's my doing, and I chastise myself for losing control. Surely, she can feel the heat, but she doesn't feel the desire that I feel. That's special. *Just for me.* Courtesy of the annoying predator within.

"I—um," she begins.

She fiddles with her thumbnail, using one to scratch the other. I wait for her to continue, but she doesn't. She's quiet for a long time before she finally speaks, and when she does, I can tell she's lost her courage. I blame myself for this. Clearly, she wanted to talk to me, and I made her so uncomfortable she shut down.

"Holland asked if I could bring him some things from my shop," she says. "But I'm . . . I'm not sure I should go alone."

"I can go with you. If—If you want."

She nods.

"I'd feel better if you were there," she admits.

She hops off my bed and walks to the door. I follow her, wondering if I should press the topic. She may have needed an escort given everything that is going on, but that's not why she came to me. There's something she wants to tell me, but she's too scared to say it. I hate to think her silence is due to fear. I may lose control around her sometimes, but I'd never hurt her.

"Luna?"

"Hmm?"

"You know you can tell me anything, right?" I ask.

With her hand on the doorknob, she looks back at me.

The look on her face is...startling. Her eyes are soft and vulnerable. She is smiling, but only slightly. She nods slowly, and as her lips part, I wait for her to say something, to confide whatever it is she's desperate to share.

But I wait for words that never come, because almost as quickly as she turned to look at me, she's leaving, walking out the door and into the hallway. Speechless.

# FIFTEEN

The street is deserted as we enter Lunar Magic.

The shop is just as I remember it, with wall-to-wall bookshelves and tables strategically staged with everything a burgeoning witch could want. During my last visit here, I noticed that Luna tends to cater to novices, because skilled witches are crafty at heart. My mother grew everything we needed, and if it couldn't be grown, she made it out of raw materials found in the woods behind our house. That's why the first time I stepped foot in her magic shop, I was already a vampire.

I inhale deeply, letting the stale scent of sage and lavender wash over me. It reminds me of home, of a past not so war-torn, but its calming effect is quickly overpowered by something much more insidious.

The bell affixed above me jingles incessantly when I close the door. I can still hear it, even though several seconds have passed.

I keep my back to the shop and eyes on the road. We're so close to the crime scene, I can still smell the blood-soaked earth. I hoped closing the door would block out the smell of dead, decaying witches, but it didn't. My senses are far stronger than thin walls, brick exteriors, and glass windows.

"What did Holland say to you about the ritual?" I ask.

Since my senses betray me, I opt for plan B and ask mindless questions. If Luna suspects anything, she doesn't mention it. She's a real trouper and responds to questions I already know the answers to.

"Nothing really," she says. "He only asked me to get a few things."

Of course, I already know this. I didn't have to be there to know what Holland would say to her. I think he trusts her more than the hunters do, but not enough to include her in on any specifics. This is Sofía's doing. Her betrayal still stings when it comes to outsiders.

The sound of her shuffling around the shop from behind me isn't distracting enough to tear my gaze away from the street or to block out the scent of blood that hangs heavily in the air. Until I became a vampire, I didn't realize how dulled human—or witch—senses are. Now, they work together. I can *hear* smells, and this one... It's loud, like a siren, and it is beckoning any vampire nearby. This is a dangerous situation to be in, considering we can't protect these people if we must defend ourselves.

"What does he need?" I ask.

Like my last question, I already know the answer to this too. After all, I was once a witch. Holland may be creating this spell on his own, but he's using previous spells and rituals to craft it. He'll need candles in specific colors and crystals with certain abilities.

"Five different crystals, the bigger the better, I guess," she says. "Some herbs, an elixir, yellow candles, and something with a pentagram."

"What about the other orb?" I ask.

If the ritual is going to work, we'll need both the Orb of

Helios and the Orb of Selene. We got lucky when Luna had the Orb of Helios, but without its partner, we'll never be able to harness the eclipse's power.

"I think Aurelia is getting that," she says.

The fact that Holland is divvying out supply lists means we're close to finishing this, and my guess is that Aurelia left around the same time we did. She's probably in town right now—sans escort. She may be the high priestess of her defunct coven, but she's not all powerful. Should a rogue attack, she may not survive. And we need her. More specifically, we need that orb. If my father wants to stop the ritual before it even has a chance, killing her and destroying the orb would be a good place to start.

My annoyance with the witches distracts me long enough to break the spell, and I turn to see Luna putting the last remaining items in a canvas shoulder bag. She strides over to me and hands me the tote. I take it on instinct.

"You should really be the one carrying this," I say, but I'm already looping the strap around my torso. "If we're attacked—"

"I'm not coming back with you," she says.

"I— Oh..."

Though her confession surprises me, I know she's making the right call. She shouldn't come back. She shouldn't be anywhere near the manor today. In fact, she should be as far away as possible. I've been so distracted by what has already happened that I forgot to worry about what could be. If we lose, he wins, and with his victory will come the downfall of Darkhaven.

"Good idea," I say. "You should leave town. Get as far away as possible."

"I— No," she says. "I'm just not coming with you *now*. I'll be there later."

"You shouldn't come at all, Luna."

She frowns, and even though I feel guilty for sounding rude and unappreciative, making her upset with me is for her own good.

"Like it or not, you need me," she says.

"What exactly can *you* do?"

My tone is intentionally harsh, and she winces. But this time, I don't feel bad about it. I never should have brought her into my world, and even though she's hurting now, she'll realize later that I was right. The hunters and I may be doomed, but she doesn't have to die today.

"You're hungry," she says. "You're *all* hungry, and without food, you stand no chance."

"You were going to the butcher?"

She nods. "And if he doesn't have anything, I'll stop by the hospital."

"You're going to steal blood bags for us?" I ask, shocked.

"Darkhaven needs you tonight. So I think the hospital can lose a few blood bags to get you all through this."

"If they catch you—"

"They won't."

"But if they do—"

"I'll run."

I can't help but smile at her. I'm not sure another person has surprised me as much as she has in the short time we've known each other. She's a good friend—better than I deserve.

"You're pretty brave for a human," I say.

A sly grin forms on her face, and she looks away. She turns toward the counter and tinkers with the stack of books piled near the cash register. She pushes a few aside to grab one at the very bottom.

"I want you to take this too," she says, handing me a large tome.

"What is it?" I ask as she slides it into my hand.

"I've been researching Darkhaven's history."

"I didn't ask you to do that."

"You didn't have to," she says. "There are places I can go that you can't, and I was willing to take the risk."

I'm not sure what it is about Luna that evokes such strong emotions from me. It could be her innocence or her tantalizing aura. Or maybe her courage and loyalty. Whatever it is, it makes her heart too damn big for this messed up world.

"What did you find out?" I ask.

"I was able to track this down," she says, pointing at the book in my hands. "It's the detailed history of Darkhaven, from beginning to now... ish. I don't think it's been updated in the last decade, but the parts about the mine are accurate."

I rub my palm over the worn leather cover, turning the book to look at the spine. A square sticker has been affixed to the bottom corner, and the tape sealing it in place is beginning to warp. There are letters and numbers in a small typeface.

I look Luna in the eyes. "Is this from the library?"

She gnaws on her lower lip and shakes her head, eyes cast downward.

I frown at her answer and rub my thumb against the faded white sticker.

"I stole it," she says softly.

"You *stole* this?"

She nods.

"I was afraid to check it out," she says quickly. "I wasn't sure who I could trust, and if the wrong person found out we were looking into the mines, well..."

"Smart thinking. We should assume my father has eyes and ears everywhere."

I slide the book into the tote and reposition the strap on my shoulder.

"There are details on several different entrances to the mines," she says. "They were supposed to be sealed off once it was shut down, but the one we found wasn't. I think there are more. Maybe you can use those to, you know, enter undetected or something."

"That might work."

"Surprise attacks *always* work," she says, smiling brightly. "You get 'em while they're distracted."

I chuckle. Maybe it is her innocence. It's been a long time since I met someone with a childlike naïvety.

"You know, I'm beginning to think I'm corrupting your virtue," I say. "Cover-ups. Theft. Murder. What's next?"

"More theft," she says with a shrug. "I doubt the butcher will have as much as we need."

"Just be careful."

As much as I hate the idea of sending Luna on her own, I don't think I could stop her, and we do need to refuel before we face my father. Still, Luna is the last person I want to sacrifice for a blood run.

"This is going to work," she says, misjudging my silence.

"Maybe. I'm a little nervous about putting everything we have into one plan. We need a reliable backup."

"You have one. The sun spell."

"I'm not so sure that will work anymore," I admit. "Without a full coven, we're asking a lot of Holland and the others."

"How so?"

"One witch can only summon so much energy before it becomes too much. That's why we gather as a coven. It makes us stronger. The stronger we are, the more we can do with our magic. What we really need is more help—more witches, more vampires, more power. A few hunters and half a coven against a rogue army . . ."

I sigh and shake my head. Even *thinking* about our slim chances hurts my heart, so I don't bother saying it aloud. I don't need to repeat what we both already know.

Luna is quiet for a long time, and I assume it's because she's as distraught as I am. Given the life we live, we are used to the anguish of death, but somehow, each loss is more painful than the last. This time, I *know* we won't all survive, and I just have to sit back and watch it happen. I have to let my friends die for the greater good.

"You have me," she says. "I'll do everything I can to help."

I smile, but I know it doesn't reach my eyes. It's a fake smile. A comfort smile. Nothing more than an emotionless, standard expression. And that makes it so much worse.

"I really appreciate everything you have done for us," I say. "But there isn't anything you can do now. Humans wouldn't survive a battle like this."

Luna nods.

"You're right," she says. "A human wouldn't last long."

Luna locks the door behind me when I leave the magic shop, and I can't help but grin. It feels like so long ago when a simple lock and key made me feel safe too.

I can feel her gaze on me as I race across the street,

desperate not to be seen or followed. My thoughts calm only when I enter the safety—and coverage—of the forest.

Even though I appreciate everything Luna is doing for us, I can't stop thinking about what will happen *after* we find a way into the mines. This book will certainly give us an advantage should we decide to fight on their turf, but its usefulness stops there.

We still don't know how to destroy the amulet without effectively causing a global apocalypse. It's simple, really. The amulet contains the power of both my former coven and the dark entity they summoned when they harnessed black magic. When released, that power will be even stronger than what I experienced when I stumbled on those dead witches. I was incapacitated then, so what will happen when everything inside the amulet is unleashed? It'll be deadly. Not just for me, but for everyone around me. And it'll spread until it consumes the world.

I know what needs to be done, but it seems impossible. Holland and the last remaining witches need to slowly release the coven's magic into the earth while the hunters and I distract the rogue army. Next, we need to contend with the entity.

The amulet was supposed to serve as a prison, keeping everyone safe, but the witches' magic amplified its power. Now that it's leaking, we have a serious problem. Keeping it separated from the world didn't work, so maybe allowing it to merge with something is the answer. But who will sign up for a suicide mission?

Our targets are obvious, and both are eager for power. If Sofia or my father absorbs the energy within the crystal, we'll have a *living* target to eliminate. A *natural* death by our hand might be the only way to defeat a *natural* darkness. Killing its host might send it back to wherever it came from.

But even though both desire power, neither want death. Convincing them to absorb the energy won't be easy. I think the only way this will work is if one volunteers. It needs to be *their* idea, not ours. Unfortunately, I think Sofía is too smart to fall for this, but my father—he might be too far gone to see how dangerous this really is.

The plan seems simple. My father absorbs the energy contained in the black onyx crystal. They merge, and the darkness takes over. I kill him, and on his way to hell, he'll take the entity with him. The coven's magic should be left behind, and Holland and the witches complete their ritual to send it back into the earth, where it will be recycled and reborn.

With my father and the amulet gone, we'll be left with two problems: his army and his lackey. If the sun spell is successful, his army will fall quickly, but Sofía will fight to survive. I just have to fight harder.

By tomorrow, the eclipse will be over. The entity will be gone. And I will have killed my father.

# SIXTEEN

The manor is eerily silent. I close the door softly and tiptoe through the foyer. The doorway to my right leads to the parlor, where I find Holland sitting on the floor, flipping through the pages of a thick tome. He's surrounded by stacks of books, just as he has been since this all began. The floor creaks under my weight, and he glances up at me.

"Did you bring everything on the list?" he asks, forgoing pleasantries.

I nod as I enter the room, clutching the strap of the bag to my chest.

From the parlor, I can see into the adjoining sitting room and conservatory. There are four witches, including Aurelia, in the sitting room. They too are sprawled on the floor, noses pressed firmly into dusty texts.

Malik catches my eye. He and the other hunters are in the conservatory. Malik is slouched forward, elbows resting on his thighs, head in his palms as he stares at the floor. Hikari is sitting beside him, hands grasping the arms of her chair in a white-knuckled grip. Jeremiah is across from her, and his knee is bobbing up and down in fast, steady thrusts. This is the first time I've seen all three hunters visibly nervous. The sight puts me on edge.

"We still need the other orb," I say.

I glance at Aurelia. Either she doesn't hear me, or she ignores my concern.

"We have them both," Holland says.

He sits upright, back straightening with confidence, as he hands me a small, rectangular wooden box.

I hold it in my hands, surprised by how light it feels. It's as though it holds nothing but air. I run my thumb over the bronze latch before opening the lid. Inside the box, there are two glowing orbs nestled safely on a cream-colored silk cushion.

When I first saw the Orb of Helios, it looked bright white, almost opalescent, but beside the Orb of Selene, its counterpart, I see now that it is golden. Representative of the moon, the Orb of Selene is truly iridescent. It's so bright and clear, I can see every swirl inside the orb.

The air is humming and buzzing with energy, and I think it's because they are together. On their own, they may have certain advantages, but like the sun and the moon, the orbs are stronger together.

"Don't touch them," Holland says.

I snap the lid shut and latch the lock. I hand him the box, and he takes it carefully.

"Wasn't planning to," I lie.

"I don't think they'd do much damage if you did, but I'd rather not risk it," he says. "Plus, the more people who touch them, the longer it'll take to cleanse, and we don't have much time."

"Speaking of time," I say. "I have an idea. A plan."

This must catch Malik's attention, because he stands abruptly and makes his way toward me. Hikari and Jeremiah follow, but the witches remain at bay. Considering that they're in the next room, they're close enough to hear, but I think they're so distracted by what they're reading that I might actually have some time alone with the hunters to work out my idea.

I slip the tote off my shoulder and pull out the book Luna stole from the library. I hand the bag to Holland but keep the book in my arms.

He peers inside and nods approvingly as he takes out the supplies one by one, carefully placing them in a line on the floor in front of him.

"You said you have a plan?" Malik asks.

"First, Luna . . . um, *found* this book," I say.

Another lie.

"It's a detailed history of Darkhaven," I say. "It has sections dedicated to the mines. There are supposed to be several more points of entry that are likely unsealed."

"And you want to enter there and attack from behind?" Malik asks.

I shake my head. "That was the original idea. But I've been thinking about it, and I don't think we'll win if we attack them on their turf."

"Agreed," Hikari says.

"We should do it here," I say. "At the manor, where we're at our strongest."

"We'll be just as strong in the mines," Malik says.

"Familiarity with your surroundings is a strength too," I remind him. "We have no idea what we're getting into down there. We'd be surrounded and unaware of which tunnel leads to freedom and which leads to a dead end."

"How will you draw them here?" he asks.

"I think I can use one of these secret entrances to lure them out."

"So you don't want us to fight there because it's too dangerous, but it's not too dangerous for you to go alone and lure them out?" Hikari asks, arching a brow.

"Getting in and out quickly isn't the issue," I say. "We can get there, and we can find them. They're not exactly hiding. But fighting inside, dodging attacks when we're surrounded and at a dead end... We'd lose. At least with me luring them out and leading them here, we'd have a chance."

"Why not use magic?" Hikari asks.

"We have to leave magic out of it," Holland says. "It'll take all our energy just to focus on the sun spell."

"The best chance we have is if I lure them out," I say. "They won't follow just anyone, but he'll follow me. My scent will lead him straight to the manor."

"And once they get here?" Hikari asks.

"All we have to do is distract them long enough for the spell to take effect."

"Remember, there's just as much of a chance that this spell will kill you too," Holland says. "We plan to target only the rogue vampires, but it's possible we won't be able to control that much power."

"That's another reason why we should do it here," I say. "Everyone, including the rogues, will be out in the open. They can't take cover in the mines then. But we can take refuge inside the manor."

"The rogues will try to come inside," Hikari says.

"Then we'll kill them," I say. "But most will perish to the sun."

"Doing this anywhere but here seems unnecessarily risky," Malik agrees.

"Where are you at with the spell?" I ask Holland.

"There's nothing more we can do," he says. "We know the ritual. We've written the spell. All that's left is to cleanse and create our circle. We can't do that part until it's time to begin."

"It sounds like all we need are the rogues," Hikari says.

"Once they get here, we won't need long before our spell takes effect," Holland says. "If it works, you'll be taking cover very quickly into the fight."

"That's good," I say. "The sooner the better."

"Right, because we're severely outnumbered, and we won't last long," Hikari says.

No one responds. By now, we're used to Hikari's brutally honest speech, but this time, when we're a breath away from beginning our ritual, it hits differently. My heart sinks at the thought of losing yet another person. When will this end? I'm running out of people for this world to sacrifice.

"Do you think you could draw them out and lead them here?" Malik asks.

"I do," I say. "He'll probably sense me before I even enter the mines."

"What about the amulet?" Hikari asks. "The sun spell might take care of the rogues, but it won't affect the crystal."

"I have an idea for that too," I say. "But it's risky."

"How so?" Malik asks.

"If my father absorbs the magic inside the entity, we would then have something physical to destroy."

"That would also destroy the entity?" Malik asks.

"I can't be sure," I say. "Hence the risk, but I think so."

"Then why can't we just smash the crystal with a brick and be done with it?" Hikari asks.

"Because the crystal is a stone prison," I say. "It is not a living host. The crystal can't die. But he can . . ."

"What about the coven's magic?" Malik asks.

"That would be released, and Holland and the others would need to send it into the earth," I say.

"Like they did earlier," Hikari says.

"Exactly like that," I say.

"If he absorbs the energy in the stone, he'll be really powerful," Holland reminds us. "Too powerful. *Unnaturally* powerful."

"But not for long," I say. "He's also rogue. The sun spell will kill him too."

"And if he's too strong even for that?" Holland asks. "Or if he absorbs the energy before we're ready?"

"I'll distract him as long as I can," I say. "It's me he wants, so it's me he'll stay focused on."

"You could die," Holland whispers.

"I know. But I'm willing to risk my life to stop him."

Malik opens his mouth to speak but immediately silences. He frowns, and his gaze darts to the large bay windows beside us. They are facing the front garden, where the stone pathway leads to the forest. The windows are stained glass, and the dark gray-and-black coloring muddles what lies beyond.

There is a figure there, but it's so blurred I can't make out details on its identity. But it's small and moving quickly, quietly. I clench my jaw shut to steady my breathing, fearful that whatever is running toward the manor can hear my panicked breath.

In unison, the hunters move toward the front door. Before I join them, I face the witches, who are huddled together on the floor in the sitting room. They cower in fear, eyes wide and teary. They know that their sister witches have died at the hands of rogue vampires—brutal, painful deaths—and they're afraid they too will perish. They might. But not right now.

I place my index finger against my lips and silently tell them to remain quiet and to stay down.

Aurelia nods as she grabs on to the hand of another witch. One by one, each witch continues the chain until all are linked. There is a swift burst of energy that flows through the room, but I'm certain only the witches and I can feel it. The hunters will never taste the sweet aura of magic.

I spin on my heels just in time to see the vampires rush outside. I join them quickly, hand on my dagger. I begin to slip the weapon free from its sheath, but I am stopped in my tracks when I make eye contact with our intruder.

Sofía.

My mind hisses her name as my blood begins to boil. I ball my hands into fists and squeeze them so tight, my nails dig into my palms, and I begin to bleed. I try to maintain my composure—I really, really do—but I am overwhelmed by fury, and for once, I *want* to let it take over. So I do. I become someone else in the name of vengeance.

I am standing before her in the blink of an eye, and her surprise shocks me. She had to have seen this coming. She may be stupid enough to come here, but she's not ignorant to how we handle revenge. Death is the only way she can make up for the damage she's done.

She throws her arms up, likely to summon her element, but I'm too fast for her. I step behind her, and with one arm wrapped tightly around her waist, I pin her in place in an ironclad grip. My other hand holds my dagger. The sharp edge of my blade is pressed firmly against her throat, and I realize I can bleed her out in seconds like this. It's fitting, considering this dagger was a gift to me from Jasik.

"Ava!" Malik shouts.

I glance at him, but I see only red. He's walking forward slowly, arms before him in caution. He's trying to calm me down, to talk me out of this, but I know he doesn't mean what he says. He speaks only as a leader, but in his heart, he wants to avenge his brother as much as I do.

When I lean in close, my nose touches her neck, and she pulls her head away instinctively, baring her neck. My fangs are throbbing painfully, desperate for a taste, but I know, if I give in now, if I do this, if I feed from her, there's no going back. I have every intention of taking her life, but not this way. Not because of my bloodlust.

It takes everything I have to break away from her. But I do it. I let her go. I loosen my grip and shove her, hard, to create enough distance between my anger and bloodlust and the traitor I would enjoy killing—a little too much.

Sofía stumbles forward, falling to the ground at Malik's feet. He stares down at her, jaw clenched, muscles strained. He too is finding it incredibly difficult to let her live.

"Please," she whispers.

I laugh, loud and hearty. My bellows are enough to break the trance she has on Malik, because he looks at me. The others stare too, and I imagine I sound manic, like a crazed psycho on the brink of another breakdown. But I can't help it. The amusement I feel while watching her beg us to spare her life is too strong to contain.

"I didn't come here to fight," she says.

"You can't possibly think we'd fall for another trap," Hikari says.

"I'm not lying," she says. "I escaped. They don't even know I'm here."

"Why would you come to us?" Malik asks. "Why not just leave town?"

"Because he'll find me," she says. "He'll hunt me every day for the rest of my life, and I don't want to spend what time I have left fearing him."

"Why would he do that?" Malik asks.

"He doesn't handle betrayal very well," she says.

My mind flashes to the last moment I was at my childhood home. He felt so betrayed by this town that he came back just to burn the home he built to the ground—with his family and coven inside.

"Even if this isn't some elaborate scheme to catch us off guard, you must have realized that we would never trust you again," Malik says.

She nods and sniffles.

"And you still came here," Hikari says. "Either this is a trap, or you're too stupid to live."

"I have information," she says. "I know his plans. I can help you."

Malik glances at me, and I groan under his stare. Sofia just spoke the magic words—the only words that might make us question killing her quickly. Now, we need her. We need information that only she can provide.

"What do you get out of this?" Malik asks.

"Revenge," she says quickly.

"Why would you need revenge?" he asks.

"Because he lied to me," she says. "He told me he would share the power inside the crystal, but he took it all for himself. He *used* me to get what I wanted, even after I proved myself worthy, and that pisses me off."

"Are you saying he merged with the crystal?" I ask.

She nods.

"He absorbed the energy inside?" I ask, still unbelieving.

"Yes, Ava," she says, tone sharp. "The amulet is gone. He has the power now."

I suck in a sharp breath but quickly press my lips together in a tight line, desperate not to show my excitement. I know I am failing miserably, but I can't help it.

Malik arches a brow at me, and I try to make him understand with my eyes. Getting my father to absorb that energy on his own was the hardest part of my plan. The sun spell, the ritual, the eclipse, even facing the army—all those things we could handle. But our plan would not work if he didn't willingly allow that energy to enter his body. Now that he did, we have something physical to kill. We actually have a chance.

"Are you okay?" Hikari asks.

"She's happy, because now she can kill her father," Sofía says.

I narrow my eyes at her, anger overthrowing my recent joy. She speaks so casually about murdering a loved one, like this is normal speech for everyone, but it's not. It's only normal for *her*, the psychopath. She massacred her coven to prove herself to my father, and even though she didn't get what she wanted, she shows no remorse. She wants revenge not for her fallen coven but for herself. Because she didn't get the power she was promised.

"That *thing* is not my father," I hiss. "Just as *you* are not my friend."

"Maybe not," she says. "But you need me. He's not stupid. He knows you'll try to kill him. But he's strong. Stronger than anything I've ever felt. Even stronger than you—the hybrid who thinks she knows all."

"Physically, he's strong," I say. "But mentally, he's weak."

"How so?" she asks.

"Because he isn't prepared to die for this war."

"And you are?"

"Enough," Malik says.

He interrupts me before I can respond, and I can't help but wonder if he was too scared to hear my answer.

"We've made it clear that we do not trust you," Malik says. "But we can use you."

"What do you want me to do?" she asks.

She stands, brushing off her dirty palms on her jeans. Beside Malik, she looks so small and fragile, but appearances are deceiving. I must never forget that Sofía is capable of murder. If she could kill someone she loved, there's no telling what she would do to us at our weakest moments.

"Lure them here," he says.

"I—I can't," she says. "How would I do that? They'd never come here just because I tell them to."

"You've already shown us that your deception knows no bounds," Malik says. "I think you're smart enough to lure them from the mines and into the woods."

"If he thinks we're together, he will come," I say.

"When this is over, you are to leave Darkhaven," he says. "Leave and never return."

Sofía swallows hard and nods. Her heartbeat is steady, and I almost believe that she has no intention of ever returning. But I know better than to trust a witch.

When this is over, if she's still alive, I will kill Sofía. If not for me or for Jasik or for our security, then as retribution for the coven she murdered.

# SEVENTEEN

I count each minute Sofía is gone, and now that I've reached thirty, I'm beginning to doubt our plan.

I'm sitting on the steps to the front porch, legs dangling down over the steps below me. Despite the many distractions, I keep my attention on the woods, searching for evidence that we are not alone.

The witches have begun cleansing for the ritual. The items Luna donated to our cause were washed in a saltwater bath while the witches themselves were saged. I'd prefer them to do the ritual inside, out of harm's way, but they need direct access to the eclipse to make their spell work.

Aurelia has begun marking the earth to form their circle. Once she has finished and the witches have entered, they will create a magical barrier to keep out vampires—rogue and hunter alike. It's similar to the spell we used during our full moon rituals. We too created a barrier to keep away vampires, and it worked well. Until it didn't.

We need thirteen witches to form a complete coven, but we have only five—one for each element, one for each point on the pentagram.

I glance at them, watching as they place sticks on the ground to outline both the pentagram and the circle around it. At each point, they place an item to represent the element of that direction.

The upper-right point of the star represents water, and there is a chalice filled with sea essence. The lower-right point is for fire, and there are matches. The upper-left point represents air, and beside it are feathers. The lower-left point is for earth, and there is a pile of dirt and crushed leaves. The final point at the very top of the pentagram represents spirit, the rarest element of all. There, Holland placed a cauldron filled with the herbs he asked Luna to bring.

On either side of each point in the pentagram, there are five yellow candles and five white candles, to represent the sun and moon, and standing directly behind the candles, there are five witches. Each witch is holding a large cluster of clear quartz crystals in their palm. Their other hand is hovering over their crystals, palms facing downward to encircle the stones. Their eyes are closed, and they are chanting in unison. Clear quartz is used to amplify the power of other objects, and their hope is that it will give us the power boost we need for a successful spell.

At the very center of the pentagram, there is a small altar. On that altar, there is a rectangular wooden box, and inside that box, there are two orbs—one for the sun and one for the moon. I stare at it, silently praying they're as powerful as we've been led to believe. Everything is riding on this spell, and it will fail if the orbs can't harness the power we need to defeat the army.

The spell seems simple. The witches will summon the power of the sun and the moon, which are overhead thanks to the eclipse. That power will flow through the orbs, and the witches will use the orbs to emit a powerful blast of sunlight. Any vampire near Darkhaven will perish under this light. They will then release that energy, and it will flow back to its natural host in the sky. The eclipse will be gone, and the war will be over . . . theoretically. Like I said, the spell is actually fairly simple, and that's what worries me. Easy doesn't come easily in this world.

I pick at my cuticles, desperate to distract myself from the overwhelming doubt and fear that's threatening to smother me. I glance at Malik, who is watching me curiously.

"Nervous?" he asks.

I shake my head. "Not even a little," I lie.

"It's been a half hour." He glances over his shoulder at the forest, and I follow his gaze.

The trees are steady. There is no movement, but I didn't expect that there would be. We may be able to make it to town and back in a half hour, but Sofía couldn't.

"She's mortal," I say. "It takes her longer to reach town."

He nods.

"Hopefully, that's—"

Malik stops and turns around to fully face the woods. I rise and stand beside him, readying myself. The trees rustle, and the sound of footsteps grows louder. There are several sets—too few to be an army but too many to be only Sofía.

Still, could she be back already? And who could be with her? I expected the traitorous witch to be an hour at least.

I look to Holland, who shares my fear. They aren't ready yet. If this is my father and his army, we need to buy time.

Luna emerges from the trees, pushing branches aside as she stumbles forward. She is holding a cooler in her hands, and my stomach growls at the sight of it. I take a step forward, prepared to greet her, when I am halted. I tense, sucking in a sharp breath. Behind Luna, a half dozen people emerge from the woods.

I open my mouth to scold her, to ask how she could be so careless to lead humans here, but I can't find the words to articulate just how pissed I am. The last time we spoke, I tried to convince her to leave town, because I couldn't promise her protection. And *this* is her answer? To bring *more* people into harm's way?

When she sees me, she stills, eyes wide.

"Don't be mad," she says quickly.

I almost laugh. I feel like a mother who has to parent a troubled teen. Except this time, her inability to follow the rules is going to get a lot of people killed.

"How could you bring them here?" I hiss.

I speak softly, as if I could chastise her in secrecy, as if the people standing directly behind her can't see or hear me.

"These are my friends," Luna says. "They want to help."

"How could they possibly help?" I ask.

"I told them about the rogue army," she says.

I sigh heavily, wondering what else she blabbed about. I don't dare look at Malik, but I can feel him. He's standing close enough for his anger to radiate off him and slam into me. This will go down as yet another mistake I've made that has endangered the nest. When will I learn that trusting outsiders never goes as planned?

"The destruction will spread to other towns if we don't stop them here and now," she says.

"Yes, we are well aware of the severity," I say. "But asking hum—"

"You said you needed help," she says. "At my shop. You said the one thing you need is help, so I brought help."

"Luna..."

My heart swells at the sight of her. She means what she

says. I can tell by her rapid speech, her sputtering heart, her uneven breath, but she must know that this is crazy. Humans fighting our war would never end well.

"I'm grateful that you care as much as you do," I say. "And I appreciate that you want to help, but you know we can't accept your offer."

"We're not as weak as we seem," she says.

"Perhaps not," I say. "But it wouldn't be right. Humans can't survive a fight like this. I can't ask these people to sign up for suicide."

Luna gnaws on her lower lip and glances over her shoulder at the others. A man is standing behind her. He looks suspiciously similar to Luna, with jet-black hair and gray eyes. His skin is etched in wrinkles, but he carries himself as though he's not as old as he appears. He has a scar that cuts through an eyebrow. It's a long, thick slash from his forehead to his nose. When Luna looks at him, he nods.

"I have a confession to make," Luna says.

I swallow hard. This is it. This is what she wanted to tell me in my bedroom but didn't have the courage to say. Or maybe she needed permission, and that man, whoever he is, just gave it to her. I glance between the two, waiting for her to look me in the eyes, to speak her truth, and when she does, I'm not prepared for what she says.

"I'm not human," she whispers.

I've become used to my world spinning out of control. I'm surrounded by chaos, fighting and bloodshed, death and brutality. Everything always happens so quickly, so I simply react. But it's my haste that often gets me into trouble. This time, I can't react. I can't speak. I can barely breathe. I am stunned silent by a confession I already knew. Deep down, I *knew* Luna wasn't human. Her essence speaks to me in ways I've never before experienced—but not just me. Malik was also bewitched by her. Still, neither of us confessed our suspicions.

If she isn't human, isn't witch, and isn't vampire, then what the hell is she?

"You need to know that my people have kept our existence a secret because we had to, not because we wanted to," she says. "I wanted to tell you. I really did. I just . . . couldn't."

"What does that mean?" I ask.

I'm not upset with her for not telling me right away, because I understand that she needed permission to tell me that she's supernatural. I wouldn't be allowed to reveal my identity to just anyone either. But we've been through so much. I've given her so many reasons to trust me, to believe in our friendship. The truth is, it stings a bit knowing she kept this secret when she's known mine all along.

"We've been ruthlessly hunted for centuries, blamed for what vampires have done," she says. "I couldn't just ignore my past with your kind."

"I—I don't understand," I say.

Something about her confession feels like a dagger to the heart. It's the way she says *your kind* and *my past.* She comes from tragedy, like me, and I above anyone else know how that can make you bitter.

"We hoped to come forward, to reveal our existence to you," she says. "But the death feuds between the vampires and witches proved you weren't ready yet. We're only telling you now because Darkhaven needs us. *You* need us . . ."

"Luna . . ." I whisper. "What are you?"

"We're always to blame," she says softly.

She glances down, kicking at the ground with her shoe.

"The wolves are always to blame." This time, she speaks so quietly, I barely hear her words, but I remember all the times our lifestyle bothered her, all the little comments she made when someone else was blamed for rogue attacks.

She's right. The wolves were always to blame.

"You're . . . a wolf?" I ask.

"I am."

"Like in the movies?"

"Not exactly. Those wolves never have self-control."

"And you do?"

"We do. We never hurt people. The animal attacks were never us."

"Do you . . . need a full moon?"

She shakes her head.

"So you can transform right now, then?"

She nods.

"And you're . . . strong?" I ask. "You can fight rogue vampires when you're a wolf?"

"We can. It's what we do when we . . . turn."

"You hunt rogue vampires?"

"Yes."

"You hunt the very creatures who forced you into darkness?"

Luna doesn't answer me. Instead, she walks forward and offers the cooler to Malik. He takes it cautiously and hands it to someone behind him—either Hikari or Jeremiah. I don't turn to see because I can't take my eyes off Luna. Everything about her looks the same, yet different. Her features are more striking than before. Her scent is more alluring. Her skin is more radiant. And the crescent moon necklace hanging at her clavicle glistens under the eclipse's light.

How could I not have known?

She hugs me, latching on tightly. I stiffen under her embrace but quickly melt into her. I close my eyes and rest my head against hers, feeling her steady heartbeat against my chest. We sit like this for several seconds before she finally speaks.

"Don't worry," she whispers. "I'll never hurt you."

My eyelids jolt open as I take in her promise. She speaks so confidently, so carefully, and as her words loop around my mind, replaying over and over again, I begin to believe her.

This isn't the shy, scared girl I rescued from rogue vampires. This isn't the weak human who tossed a jar of garlic at me, thinking it would cast me out of her shop. This is a werewolf who just promised she wouldn't use her power to hurt me. A promise like that means only one thing. Luna *can* hurt me. I may be a hybrid, but she's a wolf.

Since my transition, I've never felt like prey—until now.

# EIGHTEEN

We aren't alone.

I sense them immediately, yet still too late, because we are already surrounded. The steady thumps of several dozen heartbeats set me on edge.

Instinctively, I yank Luna to the side and pull her behind me, ready to put myself in between her and danger, but then I remember I don't have to do that anymore. Luna *isn't* human. She's another ally who can take care of herself.

My father emerges from the tree line, and Sofía is beside him. I narrow my gaze at her, but when she looks at me, her eyes are wide with fear. I actually believe her. I think she really did run away, but on the way back, she must've gotten caught. I knew leading him here would be risky, but I let her go nonetheless. I can't help but feel like that makes me a monster, despite everything she's done to deserve such a fate.

"I thought it best we finish this," he says.

"I couldn't agree more," I say.

My fake confidence actually sounds believable. The witches aren't ready yet, so now, I must do all that I can to stall his army. There's no better time for friendly banter with my homicidal father.

"I was already on my way here when I found this wretch returning to the mines," he says. "It seems loyalty means nothing to your generation."

"She's not with us," I say.

I'm not sure if this constitutes as a lie. She's not *really* with us ... right? We used her just like she once used us. But regardless, lying to him now, making him believe that she wasn't on a mission to betray him, just might save her life. Even though I have no intention of letting her live past tonight, I'm well aware that we need her right now. If she really is on our side, her magic will be useful.

"Well then, why keep her around?"

In a motion too quick for even my heightened senses, he slices his hand forward, striking Sofía in the neck. It's a clean, swift assault that easily pierces flesh and shatters bone. Her body falls to the ground, limp and headless. Luna screams from behind me, but I clench my jaw tightly. I can show no emotion.

"You're a monster," I say, seething.

"The truth, dear daughter, is you're correct," he says, smile malicious. "You're finally understanding. I *am* a monster. Your father died that night, and with his dying breath, he pledged his soul to me."

"My father would never do that."

He chuckles.

"Oh, but he did," he says. "He asked that I avenge his death, and I did. The vampires who took his mortality died by my hand, as did the witches who left him to rot."

I am so tense I tremble at the mention of my former coven. We may not have been on good terms, but no one deserves the sharp bite of burning alive. After a lifetime of grievances, death should be quick, painless.

"I know about your pathetic plan to overtake me, but you see, it will never work," he says. "Your fragile little bodies couldn't possibly summon the amount of power needed to stop me. And unfortunately for you, I have no intention of going down without a fight. Because I rather like it here. There are so many innocent people to corrupt, so many souls to conquer. And now, my darling daughter, I've come for yours."

"I'll *never* relinquish my soul to you."

"You know, I've learned something while inhabiting this creature's body," he says. "Hybrids are quite rare. So many little things, so many frustratingly intricate details need to align to create a hybrid. If I wasn't so annoyed by the complexity, I'd be awestruck at what you've created."

"You'll never take me," I say. "I'll *never* surrender my soul."

"I can assure you, I won't be leaving without it."

"You won't be leaving at all," I hiss.

He laughs, a bellow that bursts so loudly it startles the birds overhead. Their cawing grows louder, as does the fluttering of their wings. I didn't notice how many flocked to our area, each eagerly waiting for the battle of a lifetime. I used to fear crows because they symbolize impending death. But this time, I know they're here for *him*.

He catches me staring at them.

"I rather like crows," he says, glancing at some that have settled in a nearby tree. "Because when there's more than one, it's called a *murder*."

He smiles, sending chills through my body. It's an eerie, empty smile, and his lips seem to stretch from ear to ear, like an insidious Cheshire cat. It occurs to me that he looks different. Before, he *looked* like he was losing his mind, but now, after absorbing the entity inside the black onyx crystal, he seems . . . better. How can that be?

My confusion must be strewn across my face, because he

arches a brow, his curiosity taking over.

"Where's the amulet?" I ask.

"Must we waste time with pointless questions?"

"You absorbed the energy inside."

"I did. And I'll admit, I was disappointed in the witches' magic. It felt ... weak."

"And the entity?"

"I sent him away."

"You ... You sent him away? What does that mean?"

"Who do you think sent him here? When the witches came calling, surrounded by delicious swirls of dark magic, I answered—as I always do any time a soul reaches its breaking point. They were desperate. I happen to love desperation. It's rather ... delectable."

He sent him away, likely to possess another innocent victim, someone else who turns to black magic either intentionally or mistakenly. In all my years of fighting vampires, in saving humans, in protecting magic, I never once thought about what lies beyond. This isn't a war against rogue vampires. This is a war against evil, and if good doesn't win, the world will suffer.

"Now then, I hate to hasten our chat, but I'm growing bored quicker than expected," he says. "Bring him forward!"

A rogue vampire steps out from behind my father. He is tall and muscular, and his tangled, dirty-blond hair hangs raggedly over his eyes. His skin is so pale it's almost translucent, and he is covered in dark veins. He growls when we make eye contact, baring bloodstained teeth. Like the others, what little clothes he does wear are shredded.

I suck in a sharp breath when I see his hostage. Jasik is walking toward me, alive and well. He comes to a halt beside my father, but his eyes never leave me. They are filled with sorrow, with longing—the very same emotions that have haunted me since my sire was taken.

He appears to be okay, but his clothes are torn, and his skin is covered in dried blood. Even though his wounds have healed, I can only imagine the torment he sustained while living with the rogues. He probably did things he regrets just to stay alive. We'll forgive him, but will he forgive himself? I'm not so sure.

"Kneel."

My father gives his order, and Jasik complies without hesitation.

"I'm quite disappointed in you, dear daughter. You had so much potential—all ruined by this path of righteousness."

I take a step toward Jasik, eager to close the gap between us, but I stop just as quickly as I start.

My father sidesteps to stand behind Jasik and grabs a handful of his hair.

Jasik winces as my father bends his neck back a touch farther than natural.

Jasik's commitment to never taking his eyes off me has me worried. It's like he knows he's going to die, and if the fight is over, he wants me to be the last thing he sees.

I beg him with my eyes, encouraging him to fight, but he remains unmoving.

"I'm not sure what you see in him," my father says. "I can give you so much more. Power. A legion. The *world*."

"You only offer death," I say.

"Apt words."

He cradles Jasik's head in his hands and smiles at me as he jerks my sire's head a little too sharply—almost enough to snap it clean off. Jasik groans but still does not fight back.

"This is my favorite part," my father says. "The ultimatum. Join me or die. But know your refusal means you'll first watch him die, and then you'll watch everyone around you die, one by one. I'll save you for last."

I shake my head, tears burning my eyes. They threaten to spill, but I hold them back as best as I can. Still, even if they do not fall, he knows they're there. He knows how weak I am when it comes to my family.

"You have no chance," he says. "I have all the power here. Surrender, and they die quickly."

"You want power?" I ask, grinding my teeth. "I'll show you power."

The elements surge through me, and I scream as a blast of air erupts from my core. The energy slams into my father only a second later. It's clear by his reaction that he doubted my ability to overtake him, because he didn't even bother dodging my attack. Instead, the elements propelled him from where he stood, and now, he's flying through the air, landing on a few rogue vampires behind him. They all fall to the ground in a messy heap.

Beside me, Malik removes his dagger from its sheath and tosses it at Jasik. It spins in the air, landing perfectly in Jasik's outstretched hand. He grasps the handle and maneuvers it backward until it pierces the heart of the last remaining rogue vampire at his side. He combusts, returning to the earth as nothing more than ash.

Jasik crawls to his feet, teetering as he stands. Because he put on a good show of strength and defiance, I didn't realize he was this weak. Thankfully, the cooler Luna brought is stocked full of blood.

As if reading my mind, Luna opens the cooler and tosses containers at the feet of each hunter. Everyone grabs their offering so quickly, I barely catch any movement, but I do smell it. I sense *everything*. Each drop of blood consumed plays a song just for my ears. My stomach grumbles, but I ignore it as I rush Jasik a container of blood.

He falls limp at my side, and I thrust the lidless container at his mouth. He is rejuvenated with each gulp he takes. When he finishes, he is breathless. Blood is smeared across his lips, and I wipe it away with my thumb, relishing the tingling sensation that always comes with our connection.

My tears free-fall now because I realize just how much my doubt has consumed me. I was certain we would lose this fight, that I would never again know what it feels like to embrace my sire.

"There is more," I say to him.

I help him to his feet and scan the forest. We are completely surrounded, but surprisingly, no one has initiated battle. They are waiting for orders—*his* orders. I still can't believe he has them under control. It's a shame, because he could have done great things with this level of persuasion had he chosen a different path.

Quickly, I guide Jasik to the front steps to let him rest. I toss a few containers of blood in his lap.

"Be back soon, lover," I say with a wink.

He smiles before he rips off a cap and downs another drink.

By the time I turn around, my father has recovered from his blunder. He brushes the dirt off his hands with a great deal of dramatic emphasis. He is breathing heavily, jaw clenched shut. He looks at me, and I know we're out of time.

The witches have begun chanting, and even though they speak quietly, their Latin incantations echo all around me. My father hears it too, because he glances over at them, eyes narrowing. If we are to give the witches enough time to complete their spell, we need to act. Now.

I look to Luna and offer a single, sharp nod.

One by one, the members of her pack transform. It's a fast, likely painful transition that they somehow complete without a whimper. Each snap of their bones and extension of muscle sounds brutal, but they don't flinch. In fact, they make no sound at all until they're standing beside me on all fours. That's when they growl. It's a low but clear threat directed at the rogues.

They look eerily similar to regular wolves with two stark differences. Their eyes glow a bright, clear amber color, and in the darkness, it appears just as neon in color as a vampire's crimson irises. And they are unnaturally large—at least double the size of a regular wolf. I suppose they have to be freakishly large if they prey on rogue vampires.

Luna steps forward until she is right beside me. Her black fur is lush and shiny, much like her hair in her human form. She growls, keeping her eyes on the rogues surrounding us. She brushes against me, and my body tingles at the sensation.

My father is staring at her in sheer disgust, but he doesn't seem surprised by her existence. I suppose that's because he's not my father, despite the fact that I still refer to him as that. He's a monster that's been around for a very long time. He's seen a lot of things—one of which likely being the wolf. He and others like him are the reason they have been in hiding all these years.

"Take them. Now!" he shouts.

I release a blast of fire so powerful it consumes everything in front of me. The trees are lit aflame, the ground scorched. The elements burn at my innards, and I scream as I fall to my knees, unwilling to relinquish my hold on them and desperate to engulf everything I can with the power they've given me.

The blast lasts for only seconds. Maybe ten. Maybe thirty. Maybe even a full minute goes by. I've lost track, because all I can focus on is the sizzling in my gut and the deafening ring in my mind. The elements are angry, but their true anger shouldn't be because of my refusal to release them. It should be directed at *them*, at what's unnatural.

I hold on as long as I can, and when I finally release my fire magic, I slump forward, digging my palms into the warm soil. Sweat drips in steady streams down my face. Chest heaving, I stare at the earth, focusing on each granule of dirt, and beckon its aid. She grants the forgiveness I seek and begins to rejuvenate me, slowly restoring my depleted strength.

When I look up again, my heart is erratic, vision blurry, and the distorted figures of fighting vampires flash before me. My eyelids are as heavy as my breathing, but I know I cannot rest. I must keep fighting, even in a weakened state.

I push upward until I can sink back on my heels and look at the damage I caused. Everything around us is dead. The trees, the grass, the flowers. And vampires. So many dead vampires. Piles of ash blow softly in the breeze. I don't know how many I killed, but I know it wasn't enough.

The hunters square off with the remaining rogue vampires, and the wolves tear apart their enemy limb from limb.

I flinch when a hand touches my shoulder and look up to find Jasik. He offers me a container of blood, and I happily drink it.

My legs are wobbly as I stand, and I lean against him. With every second that passes, I begin to feel better. My mind clears, my breathing steadies, and my stomach silences. A familiar wave of comfort washes over me, but that feeling doesn't last long.

My father is only a few feet from me, and he's rushing this way. Half of his face is burned beyond recognition, and the black-and-red blisters are seeping blood. He is walking with a limp, leaving a crater in the soil as he drags one of his feet.

"Go!" I shout as I push off Jasik.

I teeter slightly as I stand on my own, but since my strength is already returning, I brush it off quickly. Between the blood and the earth's magic, I will be restored in no time. And by the looks of him, my father won't put up much of a fight. I can take him alone.

"I won't leave you," Jasik says.

"They need you more than I do!"

The pain that flashes across his face pierces my heart, but I shake off the guilt. I can't worry about his feelings right now—not when we have a good chance of winning this fight. And by the looks of it, we *are* winning.

I glance over my shoulder at the witches. They are deep into the ritual now. Their eyes are glossed over, and their mouths are moving so rapidly, I can't even make out what they're saying. The orbs are beginning to glow, so I know I don't have much time. I must kill him before their spell takes effect. Otherwise, he'll escape while we seek sanctuary in the manor. I can't risk unleashing him on the world.

Dagger in hand, I run at my father, bypassing each swing of his arms as though they're moving in slow motion. When he brings his right arm back again, he leaves too big an opening for me, and I take advantage of it.

I spin my dagger in my palm until the blade is pointing toward me and not at him. I then twist my wrist and thrust my hand forward. My blade plunges into his chest, planting deep into his torso. I hear the exact moment his heart is severed. He stumbles backward as blood pours from his mouth.

He gasps for breath, sputtering unrecognizable words. He grabs at my blade, moaning as he tries to remove it from his chest.

I wait for him to turn to ash. One second. Then two. Then five. Then ten. Still, he remains.

He stills, and I think this is it. This is the moment my father dies . . . by my hand. But instead, he just laughs. He *laughs*.

I freeze as he removes my dagger, gripping it firmly in his hand as he turns the blade on me.

"When will you understand?" he asks. "I am *not* your father. I may have his face, his features, his memories, but I'm not some weak vampire, little girl."

He tosses the dagger into the air, catching it by the tip of the blade. He turns and whips it away from us. Steady swooshing sounds echo in my mind as it slices through the air. Until it stops. Until it is rooted in the back of the closest hunter.

Hikari shrieks as she falls to her knees. She curses under her breath—a nearly silent, angry exclamation—as she slumps forward. The rogue vampire she was sparring with takes advantage of her weakened state and charges her.

But Hikari anticipated this—as any expert hunter would—and she reaches behind her back, quickly dislodges the dagger, and plunges it forward. The rogue's surprise brings a smile to her face—just before they both combust.

Watching Hikari die forces another painful burst of magic from my body. It escapes quickly, rolling outward in all directions, heavy and thick, like the fog coming in. My remaining allies must have sensed the power surge. They retreat quickly, but nearby rogues aren't as lucky.

Unlike last time, it passes quickly, and when it's over, my father strides toward me. Though his face is scarred by my magic, his limp is gone, and I can't help but wonder if he too was putting on a show. I surrendered my weapon, and he used it to murder my friend. My magic is all I have now, and even that has been depleted.

I look to the others, who have once again initiated battle with the rogues who remain. There are still so many of them. Too many. I only have so many magical bursts available to me. I'm quickly approaching a burnout that only rest and passing time can cure.

I think he knows this. He's waiting for me to exhaust all my power on his army, leaving myself at the mercy of his reign. Without a weapon and with weakened magical power, I freeze, unsure of what else I can do.

He doesn't die. He withstands elemental burst after elemental burst. My air magic landed him on his ass, but that's it. My fire scorched his skin, but that's all. My fury is not enough, so what can I do? What will it take to kill him?

My gaze lands on Sofía's charred remains. I find myself drawn to the raw, gaping wound where her head should be. He decapitated her without a thought, and he planned to do the same to Jasik had I not intervened. Both times, he went straight for the head, as if that's the only method he relies on.

I meet his gaze, and his grin falters. He stops moving when he's only a few feet away from me. He eyes me carefully, scanning the length of my frame. I am no longer trembling, no longer scared.

Because I know how to kill him.

This time, *I* smile.

I pounce quickly, using magic to propel myself overhead. He lunges, but I'm already lifting myself upward, flipping in the air until I stand behind him. I land quietly, gracefully. I know he still hears me, but I am too fast for him. I leap forward, jumping onto his back and wrapping my legs around his torso. I cling tightly, squeezing my thighs together in an ironclad grip. I link my heels together, trapping his arms beneath my legs, and as he struggles to free himself, we fall to the ground.

I grab onto his head with one arm, digging my hands into his thick, salt-and-pepper hair. My nails dig at his scalp, drawing blood. I grip his shoulder with my other hand. I push his torso down as I lift his head up, and his screams are so loud, it stops the rogues in their tracks.

They watch as I rip his head from his body.

When I finally stand, his body is unmoving, and his head is in my hand. It dangles in the air from his hair. His eyes are wide, lifeless, and his jaw is agape. I turn to face the rogues and chuck what's left of their leader at their feet. It combusts just before it reaches them.

I step forward, readying myself for another battle, but I am stopped by Holland's screams. The orbs are glowing so brightly, it burns my eyes to even look at them. I scream for the others to get inside, and one by one, the remaining hunters scurry to the manor. The wolves stay outside, surrounding what's left of my father's legion. If they wish to run, they'll have to fight.

I slam the door shut just as a blast of sunlight reaches us.

When it's over, we open the door, shielding our eyes from the sunlight. We remain inside, clinging to the shadows, but from our viewpoint, we can see the sky is bright, the air is clear, and the eclipse is over.

The witches tend to the wolves, who are now lying nude in the yard. With the eclipse gone, the moon no longer holds her sway, and they are in human form.

Holland removes his jacket and places it on Luna's shoulders. When she stands, I can see that her body is covered in claw marks, but she's no longer bleeding. In the time it takes to slip her arms into the jacket sleeves, some of the gashes have already healed.

She takes the steps slowly until she reaches the doorway. Her eyes are bright and shiny, and her tantalizing aura offers just enough happiness for the rest of us to feel her ecstasy.

"We did it!" she exclaims as she pulls me into a hug.

We did. We really, really did.

# EPILOGUE

Dear Diary,

I've decided to start journaling, because eternity is a very long time—and I want to remember everything.

It's been one month since we beat my father's rogue army, sending them all straight to hell. Sometimes, I still think about him, choosing to remember the good, honest, kind man he used to be and not the monster he became. It's funny, because we both feared death in our final moments, and we both tried to avoid it. He turned to darkness, but I found light. Asking Jasik to save me that night ended up being the best decision of my life.

Speaking of my sire, he still hasn't forgiven himself for what happened. He burdens himself with guilt not meant for him, because what happened wasn't his fault. But he'll never see it that way, because for the better part of a thousand years, no one bested him—until her. Until Sofía. He's slowly starting to trust his instincts again, and every once in a while, the confident, sweet man I fell in love with shines through. I know I'll get him back . . . eventually.

We still haven't gone into Hikari's bedroom. It's almost like the door is sealed shut, forever untouched. I like to think we're leaving it the way she left it, the way she wanted it to be kept. One day, we might go inside, clean it out, maybe invite another hunter to join our nest. But that day won't be anytime soon.

We added her tombstone in the garden cemetery. We put her right beside Amicia. I like to think that she's watching us now, and she's smiling.

Malik and Luna have taken things to the next level. She officially moved into the manor. That night she showed up out of the blue with a cooler full of blood, I thought she might have hexed us all. Turns out, she only bewitched Malik, who hasn't loved anyone in this way for a long, long time. I'm happy for them, and I'm even happier it's her. Luna's more than a friend. She's family.

Speaking of family, the wolves basically live here now too. At least, it feels like they do. The sun spell wreaked havoc on the manor, and they've been helping us restore it to its former glory. It helps to have self-sufficient friends who know their way around tool bags. We've also planted trees. Lots and lots of trees. One day, when they're big and tall and lush, I'll look out my window, and I won't see the devastation of magic. I'll see the beauty.

The humans of Darkhaven are suspicious. My father's army wasn't discreet, and the bodies he left behind caused more questions than answers. The witches did their part, spreading false narratives about deadly animal attacks, but they never once mentioned wolves. Eventually, I think humans will discover the truth, but now that everyone's working together, that day won't be for a very, very long time.

Yesterday, we hosted a barbecue, and everyone came— Luna's pack, Aurelia's new coven, Malik's nest, and, of course, Holland. We warmed blood for vampires and grilled meat for the eaters—Ha! (Mental note: call them eaters in person to get a reaction and write about it later. I bet it'll be funny!)

The gathering was strange. I grew up surrounded by people. Witches were everywhere, all the time, but it never felt like . . . home. I always felt out of place and in the way. Not anymore. Not with them. Who would have thought it took death for me to find my true family?

While everyone ate and talked and laughed, I just took it all in. The realization hits me hard sometimes. We fought for so long, and we lost so much. But in the end, we won. The war is over, and Darkhaven is finally at peace. Turns out, all it took to bridge the gap between vampires and witches was to add some wolves to the mix. Who knew?!

"Are you ready?"

I glance up from my journal to find Jasik leaning against the bathroom doorframe to our bedroom. His arms are crossed, hair still wet, and droplets of water are dripping down his skin.

I hop off the bed and tuck the notebook into our bedside table. He smiles as I stride over to him.

"What?" I ask, a sly smile forming.

"You're just so beautiful."

With my hands on his chest, fingers bunching the fabric of his shirt, I pull him down to me. The moment his lips touch mine, I'm lost in his embrace. My very soul quivers with lust, with a deep desire only he can fulfill. When we pull apart, we are needy and breathless.

I lean against him, resting my head on his chest. His heartbeat is steady beneath his shirt, and I close my eyes to the lull of each methodical thump. I inhale deeply, taking in his scent. He smells so safe, so familiar, like mint and vanilla and blood.

"What are we doing today?"

I ask him this every day, even though the answer never changes. Now that the war is over, our schedules are far laxer. There is no need for nightly patrols or family meetings about lurking rogue vampires. Gossip spreads fast and far in the vampire world, and the word is out. My father is dead. His army is gone. And anyone coming to Darkhaven looking for trouble will find just that.

With nothing but peace on the horizon, eternity sounds spectacular.

"We can do anything we want, my love."

# ALSO BY DANIELLE ROSE

## DARKHAVEN SAGA

*Dark Secret*

*Dark Magic*

*Dark Promise*

*Dark Spell*

*Dark Curse*

*Dark Shadow*

*Dark Descent*

*Dark Power*

*Dark Reign*

## PIECES OF ME DUET

*Lies We Keep*

*Truth We Bear*

For a full list of Danielle's other titles,
visit her at DRoseAuthor.com

# ACKNOWLEDGMENTS

Writing a novel is no easy task, especially when the idea behind said novel becomes a nine-book series. Thankfully, I am blessed with having many inspiring and supportive people in my life, and I absolutely wouldn't have made it as far as I did without them.

To Shawna, my writing cohort—you are such a special person and the very best friend a girl could ever ask for. Thank you for the midnight rants, the writer's block chats, and the daily meme chuckles. Cheers to another book!

To my family—your unwavering support while I pursue a professional writing career means everything to me. I love you all so very much.

To the readers and members of my Facebook group, Petals & Thorns—I adore you all so very much, and I hope the Darkhaven Saga has brought you as much joy as it has brought me. This one is for you.

Finally, to the amazing team at Waterhouse Press—your support and encouragement means more than I could ever explain. While writing this series, personal tragedy struck, but you stood by me and this series. Thank you for giving me a chance to finish it.

# ABOUT DANIELLE ROSE

Dubbed a "triple threat" by readers, Danielle Rose dabbles in many genres, including urban fantasy, suspense, and romance. The *USA Today* bestselling author holds a master of fine arts in creative writing from the University of Southern Maine.

Danielle is a self-professed sufferer of 'philes and an Oxford comma enthusiast. She prefers solitude to crowds, animals to people, four seasons to hellfire, nature to cities, and traveling as often as she breathes.

Visit her at DRoseAuthor.com

Printed in Great Britain
by Amazon

18385998R00119